Dead Village

Holly Copella

In loving memory of Carl L. Morris

ACKNOWLEDGMENTS

Copella Books: First Paperback Edition 2015
Cover Artist: Daniela
SelfPubBookCovers.com/Daniela
Printed by CreateSpace, An Amazon.com Company

PUBLISHER'S NOTE

Chapter One

$\mathcal{F}$ox Ridge Village was a small town located at the base of a hillside surrounded by thick woods. Beyond the thick woods, at the top of the hill, sat a majestic resort hotel seemingly out of place. It was late spring and the small town appeared oddly quiet despite the prelude to the upcoming bustle of summer tourist season. The winding backroad leading from town was painstakingly well-maintained with an old-world country charm. The road led to a once immaculate, massive covered bridge, which now lie in ruins in the ravine just one mile outside town. The bridge was the only way across the wide, deep ravine, leaving the town and hotel cut off from the rest of the world. The destruction of the bridge to the small town was at the very least devastating.

Two men riding al-terrain vehicles stopped just before the demolished covered bridge. There was a sawhorse on either side of the detached road containing a blinking light and a 'bridge out' sign. Anderson looked at Carter and shook his head.

"Jesus," Anderson said with surprise as his eyes widened at the sight before them. "They said the bridge was out. No one mentioned exploded."

"This wasn't weather related," Carter replied while sharing his friend's concern. "This was intentional."

"Should we go back to town and warn them?"

"They were already out here and saw it," Carter remarked. "I'm sure they have a pretty good idea what happened already. Mayor Dino probably just doesn't want to alarm anyone. We have a long ride ahead of us." He looked down the fifteen-foot drop to the shallow stream below. "We'd better find an easier place to cross the ravine."

"It's not nearly as steep back fifty yards," Anderson informed him. "The path is narrow, so you should probably follow at a safe distance."

Carter nodded. Anderson turned his ATV and drove carefully along the narrow path alongside the treacherous ravine ledge. His four-wheeler nearly slid off the ledge. He kept the ATV from sliding into the ravine then stopped a few yards ahead to make certain Carter was able to navigate the narrow pass. When he looked back, Carter was gone! Anderson dismounted his ATV and hurried along the narrow path to where he had nearly slid into the deep ravine himself. He looked into the ravine, half expecting to see the crashed ATV, but neither Carter nor his vehicle were at the bottom. Anderson was relieved but puzzled. He looked around then hurried back along the path toward the bridge. Carter's ATV sat before the sawhorse where he had originally left him. The four-wheeler was still running. Anderson nervously looked around.

"Carter?"

There was no response. Anderson swatted a bug on his neck and gave it a flick. He took a step toward the woods. Everything suddenly became blurry. He attempted to remain on his feet but lost consciousness and collapsed to the ground.

✝

$\mathcal{I}$t was late afternoon in the alarmingly quiet town of Fox Ridge Village, which consisted of several homes and businesses. Most appeared abandoned and boarded up. There were no children playing outside on the warm, sunny day. Cars remained parked in front of several homes with a thick layer of yellow pollen covering them. None appeared to have been moved in days or longer. The town was eerily void of life. The faint sound of a gavel pounding a table within Town Hall broke the silence. The small Town Hall building contained nearly the entire population of slightly over one hundred townsfolk, all adults, crammed inside its old walls. Those living within the summer resort town were all that remained during off-season. Some were longtime locals while most were seasonal resort employees who chose to live year-round in the quaint town. Four council members sat at the folding table toward the front as commotion filled the small hall of standing room only. A man in his late forties with sturdy features, Mayor Dino Marlin, pounded the gavel to the table with a look of irritation. His shaved head and muscular build immediately gave one the impression of a former Marine. His serious look as he banged the gavel was frightening, but no one acknowledged him or the banging. The commotion continued among the townsfolk.

"Look at the idiot banging the gavel," Dino shouted above the rising commotion. "It means quiet. To you idiots who don't get it, it means shut the hell up!"

The commotion immediately ceased and all eyes were suddenly on the mayor. He was obviously well respected or possibly mortally feared.

"The bridge is out, and we've lost power and communications with the real world four days ago from the last storm we had." He inhaled deeply while looking around the crowded hall. "I know we're all under a lot of stress, but that doesn't mean we have to lose our heads," Dino informed his fellow townsfolk. "Anderson and Carter took their little four-wheeled thingies to civilization. I'm sure this will all be straightened out by morning."

"Morning?" Reed, a recent transplant to town, demanded. "We have no electricity, no heat, and the water looks like some freakish science experiment." All eyes were on Reed. He didn't seem the type to be easily ruffled, so his concerned outburst gained plenty of attention from the others. "Not to mention the strange things we've been hearing at night."

"I know most of you are fairly new to our town, but you're in the country now," Dino casually informed them. "What you're hearing is probably just animals celebrating mating season." His sly grin was almost enough to calm them. "I assure you, it's nothing to worry about."

A prudish looking woman in her late thirties, Felicia Kale, shook her head. The alarm on her face was troubling. "Be sensible, Mayor. I've lived here most of my life, and I've never heard anything like that before," she informed Dino.

Another man, Scott, quickly interjected, "Something destroyed the old bridge, and it certainly wasn't the weather that did that. It looks like it'd been blown apart."

"I think we're allowing our imaginations to get ahead of us," Dino informed them. "Let's just keep calm. Everything will be fine in a couple of days."

A stunningly handsome man in his late twenties, Tyson Marlin, stood from the front row and looked from the council to those filling the room. "Although the hotel's phones are out as well, it still has power, and Sonya said the water was clean there," he announced firmly. "Everyone's upset about the strange happenings and with good reason." He looked at Dino behind the table. "We can't spend another night in darkness and without water and heat, Uncle Dino."

"Hey, that's Mayor Dino," Dino quipped then looked around Town Hall. "We asked Mr. Waverly to attend this emergency meeting, but not surprising, he hasn't been kind enough to grace us with his presence."

"In the two years he's managed the hotel, I don't think he's ever left," Tyson said. "The hotel doesn't open for another couple of weeks. There's no reason why we can't move up there until help arrives. Most of the town works there, for God's sake. It shouldn't be an issue."

"We can't just commandeer the hotel," Dino informed Tyson while sternly raising his brows.

"Maybe Sonya can use her--" Tyson began.

Dino glared at Tyson with a look that immediately silenced the handsome young man. "Stop that sentence, if you know what's good for you," Dino growled with limited patience. "That's my niece and your sister."

Tyson frowned and returned to his seat alongside his sister, Sonya. He folded his arms across his chest with obvious annoyance to being scolded in front of the entire town. His younger sister was the female version of him except with strawberry blond hair rather than sandy brown. She grimaced, having felt his pain, and affectionately patted his arm.

A young, attractive blonde woman in her mid-twenties, Gemma Vales, stood from mid row. She appeared apprehensive. "I'll talk to Mr. Waverly on the town's behalf."

Dino glanced at the other three members at the table. All three nodded their approval. He looked back at Gemma and smiled. "Thank you, Gemma. That's very kind of you."

A firm, commanding voice was heard from the back of Town Hall. "Where would this council be without the solicitation of young, attractive women to do their dirty work?

All heads turned toward the back of the hall. A well-dressed, distinguished man of small stature in his late forties, Ravin Waverly, leaned against a support beam. As all eyes fell upon him, he casually straightened.

Dino leaned back in his chair and cocked his head to one side. A slight smirk crossed his face. "Well, it was nice of you to join us, Mr. Waverly."

"The hotel is my responsibility, but I see no reason to not accommodate the town residents at the hotel for a few nights as long as it's left in the same condition," Ravin informed them. Despite his accommodating announcement, he stood rigid and seemed disapproving. "I suggest, Mayor, the next time you have a problem that concerns me, you come to me rather than summoning me like your servant."

Ravin turned and left the hall as mysteriously as he had appeared. Several murmurs were heard as he left and quickly increased to almost deafening levels. Dino again banged the gavel to the table. This time the murmuring voices didn't cease.

Chapter Two

The Fox Ridge Village Hotel and Resort was even more impressive up close. The massive five hundred-room hotel looked more like a mansion than a hotel. There was a nine-hole golf course toward the back of the sprawling resort grounds, a small pool with hidden hot tubs on both sides, and a tennis court. The larger in ground pool was enclosed beyond a wall of glass within the hotel itself. The once immaculate landscaping was obviously in need of attention after the long, harsh winter. Pampered guests enjoyed the solitude and first-class amenities the resort offered. In addition to a world-class spa and well-appointed fitness center, the resort was known for scenic hiking, stunning views, and encounters with rare wildlife.

The hotel dining room was massive and elegant with enough room for almost any sized reception or conference. It was obvious the hotel needed a good cleaning prior to tourist season, but it was still impressive. Platters of mostly finger foods were set on one of the buffet tables. Most of the townspeople gathered in the dining room for a simple yet varied dinner. Ravin walked the room without socializing, looking more like a schoolteacher supervising his classroom. Despite being the general manager since the hotel opened two years ago and his live-in status, he almost seemed out of place in his own hotel. It wasn't clear if he was actually antisocial or socially awkward. Sonya Marlin approached Ravin.

"This was a very nice gesture on your behalf, Mr. Waverly," Sonya said while flashing a radiant smile of excessively white teeth. She was a ravishing beauty by any standards. "It reminds me of when the town used to have its annual church picnics."

"I haven't heard anything about church picnics," he remarked with some surprise. "I wasn't even aware there was a church in town."

"Once the hotel was built, most of the locals moved away and the hotel staff moved in," she informed him. "No one went to church anymore. The church burned down only a month or two after the hotel opened, and it was just left in ruins. Didn't seem necessary to rebuild it."

"Oh, the ruins by the old cemetery?" he asked.

"Yes, that was the church," she replied. "I don't know why it was never demolished."

"Wasn't there some speculation about that fire?" he asked. "Arson, as I seem to recall."

"I don't think the insurance ever paid out," she replied. "It could have been arson, I suppose. I know the property went up for auction last year. I think the hotel owner bought it." She considered her own comment. "I think the hotel owner bought a lot of property in town over the last two years."

"I believe so," Ravin replied. "The buildings have been going to waste, and I know more of our seasonal staff would like to live in town. I'm sure he intends to make repairs and rent the buildings out to the workers."

Ravin glanced across the room toward the bar. Sonya's father, Cody Marlin, poked around behind the bar, obviously looking for something stronger than punch and lemonade. Ravin was suddenly distracted. Sonya continued to talk, but it was obvious Ravin hadn't heard a word she'd said. He looked at her, as if realizing she was still talking, and attempted a polite smile.

"Will you excuse me?" Ravin asked.

She uncertainly nodded but seemed surprised by his need to leave so quickly. It was possibly the longest conversation anyone ever had with the reclusive resort manager. Across the room, Felicia stood with Darlene and watched Ravin walk away from Sonya.

"That girl is something else," Felicia huffed.

Darlene glanced across the room to see whom Felicia was referring. She looked puzzled. "Sonya?" she asked. "What do you mean?"

"She's always flirting with some man," Felicia retorted. "She's had a tarnished reputation since her early teens. You'd think that father of hers would put a stop to her behavior, but he's too busy drinking himself stupid to even care."

"Don't start with that again," Darlene said with a defeated sigh. "We're living in the modern age, Felicia. Women are entitled to have sex out of wedlock nowadays."

She glared her disapproval at the woman alongside her. "It's disgusting," Felicia informed her. "Respectable women shouldn't give in to men's sexual urges."

Darlene shook her head and gave up on the conversation. "Yes, it's sad we're not all perfect."

Reed approached Cody, who continued to search behind the bar for any sign of hard liquor. Reed casually sat on one of the barstools and watched the man intent on finding alcohol.

"You know," Reed announced, "they remove all the alcohol before they close for the winter."

"Wishful thinking," Cody muttered and leaned on the bar across from Reed. Cody was almost as good-looking as his son, Tyson. His moderately muscular build was impressive, although nowhere near as impressive as his brother, Dino. "How's the buffet?"

Reed shrugged. "Can't say I'm hungry," he replied then frowned. "I should have made the trip with Anderson and Carter. You know they can't find their way out their own driveways without me."

"So why didn't you go?" Cody asked.

"My quad hasn't been running right, and I never got around to finding the problem," he replied. "I would have just slowed them down if it gave me trouble."

"Look on the bright side," Cody announced cheerfully. "With Anderson gone a day or two, it gives you more time to win over Darlene."

Reed laughed softly and shook his head. "You really haven't been paying attention, have you?" he remarked. "Your brother's had his sights on Darlene since last fall. It's only a matter of time before he makes his move. When he does, she's jumping at the offer. Neither of us stands a chance."

"Dino isn't the take a wife and settle down type," Cody replied, although he appeared humored by Reed's assessment. "Sure, he likes her, but he'll never act on his desire."

Reed considered the comment and casually glanced across the room at Darlene, who helped Sonya mix punch. His grin indicated the thoughts he was entertaining.

Ravin approached Gemma, who stood near the buffet table with an empty paper plate in her hand. She either wasn't hungry or lacked interest in the offerings. As Ravin approached, Gemma fidgeted and acted as if she hadn't seen him heading toward her until he was alongside her. She cast a look at him, forced a smile, and then put more of an effort into sizing up the buffet. Something about his presence made her uncomfortable. If he had noticed, he didn't draw attention to it, although he seemed hesitant to speak.

"This is nice, huh?" she said and appeared to cringe at her own words. It sounded too much like the sort of small talk someone made while uncomfortable, and she seemed to realize how false it sounded.

He was equally tense and fidgeted. "Yes," he replied without sincerity. Ravin seemed almost as uncomfortable around her as she was in his company. "Gemma, I know it's off-season and you're not working, but I was wondering if you'd do me a favor," Ravin said timidly.

She finally made eye contact and turned professional with renewed confidence. "Yes, of course, Mr. Waverly. What can I do for you?"

"Would you help me do inventory of the wine cellar?" Ravin asked and masked his frown. His eyes strayed to Cody behind the bar. "Cody's been sniffing around the bar. Obviously, nothing's been stocked, but it won't be long before he finds his way to the wine cellar. I don't need him drunk."

"I understand, trust me," Gemma announced firmly with a defeated sigh. "He's all hands when he drinks."

Ravin appeared a little surprised by the comment then immediately became uncomfortable. "Please finish your dinner," he said timidly and indicated her empty plate. "You can join me in the wine cellar when you're finished."

She returned the empty paper plate a little too quickly to the stack and smiled more naturally at her boss. "I wasn't really hungry anyway."

He seemed a little surprised by her reaction then attempted a smile and nodded. "Okay then--"

t

$\mathcal{T}$he massive, modern wine cellar was filled with elegant racks containing hundreds of bottles of wine from floor to ceiling. Gemma knelt on the floor and marked items down on a clipboard while Ravin stood a few feet away from her and counted bottles. Their work was awkwardly silent. Ravin didn't appear to notice, but Gemma was obviously bothered by the silence. She glanced at him sheepishly several times from her position on the floor. It was difficult to tell what was going through her mind as her eyes swept over him. Ravin was very distinguished and refined, more so than anyone else in their little town. He was always well-dressed and his clothing were obviously expensive and of fine taste. Gemma attempted to mind her own business, but as she glanced at him several times, it seemed her curiosity was getting the best of her.

"I was, uh, wondering," Gemma announced softly and broke the silence between them. "Why didn't you ask Sonya to help with inventory?"

Despite his preoccupation with his work and preference to silence, Ravin hesitated and looked at her. Her question had peaked his curiosity. "Sonya? She works housekeeping. You're my office help. Why would I ask her?"

Gemma casually shrugged, although it came off stiff, and now avoided looking at him. "She's always flirting with you, so I just assumed--"

He suddenly interrupted her, startling her. "She only flirts with me because she thinks I control promotions, which I don't," Ravin replied a little too quickly. "I know when I'm being played, and I don't appreciate it."

Gemma immediately fidgeted and seemed embarrassed for having initiated such a personal conversation with the excessively private recluse. Ravin wasn't someone anyone really spoke with on a personal level. He mostly kept to himself and seemed to prefer it that way.

"I'm sorry," she quickly replied, minded her clipboard, and attempted to smooth things over. "I thought you two had something going on--" She immediately cringed, having realized she said the last part aloud. Gemma avoided looking at him in an attempt to hide her embarrassment.

He stared at her even though she didn't look up from her clipboard. Her reddened cheeks were a dead giveaway as to why she didn't look up. Ravin was reserved, which was putting it mildly, and she'd embarrassed herself with her comment.

"You actually thought she was interested in me?" Ravin asked with surprise.

Gemma still appeared unable or unwilling to look up and quickly shrugged it off. "Well, sure," she replied a little too quickly and in a pitch that was higher than normal. "We don't get many sophisticated, intelligent men around here, so why wouldn't she be interested in you? This town has far too many cowboys like Dino in it."

Despite that she didn't look up, Ravin continued to stare at her. It seemed a thousand thoughts crossed his mind to what was obviously meant to be a compliment. The faint sounds of screaming from somewhere upstairs broke the awkward silence. Both looked to the ceiling with surprise.

"Stay here," Ravin ordered then ran from the wine cellar to check on the situation.

Gemma was stunned by his sudden departure. She sprang to her feet and ran after him. Whatever had happened, she obviously didn't want to be alone in the wine cellar.

✝

*G*emma and Ravin ran along the main corridor toward the dining room and slowed as they approached the open doors. Gemma nervously followed Ravin inside. Both suddenly stopped and were horrified by what they saw. Out of the one hundred or so people within the dining room, nearly seventy men and women lie slumped over tables or lie on the floor alongside overturned chair. The foul stench of vomit seemed to fill the room. The nearly thirty remaining townsmen and women stood nearby or attempted to assist the fallen. Most just stared at the sight with looks of horror on their faces. Dino checked on several of the fallen people then looked at Ravin with horror.

"They're dead," Dino gasped.

Gemma gasped with horror, turned to Ravin, and clung to him to keep from looking at the mass death surrounding them. Ravin stared and appeared almost frozen.

"They--they just started gasping and throwing up then fell over," Sonya said while sobbing as her hands trembled. She clung to her shoulders to keep her hands still. "One after another."

Ravin released Gemma and approached one of the dead men. He glanced at the man's face and hands. There was purple tingeing along his lips and nail beds. The expression on Ravin's face was hard to read. Horror swept over him.

"They've been poisoned," Ravin gasped softly. "There's tingeing around the fingernails and lips."

"Poisoned?" Dino said and seemed almost unable to comprehend the words. "Are you saying the food was tainted?"

"No, this wasn't an accident. These people were murdered," Ravin replied firmly then stared at Dino while shaking his head with realization. "We have to seal off this room until the police get here."

Sonya nervously stared at her fingernails while trembling then looked at her father, Cody. "Daddy, what if the rest of us were poisoned as well?"

Cody didn't have an answer.

"It's fast acting," Ravin informed her. "You'd be showing symptoms by now." He turned to Dino. "We need to get the police out here right away."

Dino only considered his comment for a second then nodded in agreement. "It'll be a long hike, but we'll send two men out," Dino announced then looked around the room at the other survivors. "No one touches anything!"

Judging by the looks on the remaining faces, they weren't even considering it.

Chapter Three

*R*eed and Scott walked across the massive resort grounds and headed into the woods with their backpacks slung firmly over their shoulders. The trek through the woods to Fox Ridge Village was faster than taking the long, winding road. Dino and Ravin stood just outside the hotel's main entrance and watched the two men until they disappeared into the distance woods. They shared looks of concern with the hope that this would bring about an end to the horror they'd already witnessed. Once the two men were safely away from the resort, Dino and Ravin entered the hotel lobby and shut the doors behind them. Ravin groaned softly and sank against the door. Dino had a frown chiseled on his hard face.

"I suppose we wait," Dino answered the silent question in Ravin's groan. "You locked the dining room so no one can disturb anything until the police arrive, right?"

"Yes," Ravin muttered softly. "No one should eat anything that isn't sealed in a can. We can't take any chances until we know what was poisoned."

"The water," Dino gasped softly then cocked his head in question while staring at Ravin. "With all the storms we've been having lately, it's possible that something contaminated the water and that's what killed the others. That would explain a lot, don't you agree?" He suddenly grinned, shook his head, and almost appeared relieved. "We're probably overreacting over nothing. Certainly a better theory than believing a mass murderer is running around the hotel. Maybe we should tell the others."

"You can wish that all you want, Mayor," Ravin informed him with little enthusiasm as he straightened. "Contaminated water didn't kill those people."

Dino was seemingly crushed by Ravin's refusal to pretend what happened was purely accidental. "You realize what you're saying, right?"

"Yes, I do," Ravin replied while frowning. He fidgeted while attempting to maintain his refined dignity. He failed. "Someone here poisoned nearly seventy people." The look on his face was grim. "To think they're going to stop there would be a mistake."

All expression drained from Dino's face. "Do you really believe that? Do you actually think someone here, one of my neighbors, is capable of something so dark and sinister?"

"It doesn't matter what I believe. The body count speaks for itself." He sank into thought then looked at Dino. "You know, it wouldn't be a bad idea to keep everyone rounded up," Ravin informed him. "Safety in numbers."

"And yet seventy people were poisoned while together in the same room right under our noses," Dino informed him with little enthusiasm.

"Yes, but now we know what we're up against," Ravin replied with slightly more optimism. "If he wants the rest of us, he'll be outnumbered."

"You're right," Dino announced then inhaled deeply and stood proudly. He was once again the man in charge. "No one should go anywhere alone. I'll assemble everyone in the lounge. You keep them rounded up while I locate the rest."

"You'll find that some of the women have already locked themselves in their rooms after what happened in the dining room," Ravin informed him. "Some of them were pretty shaken up. I'll pull up the list of guestrooms and who's staying in which rooms from the front desk computer."

"I'll have Tyson go room to room and bring down any stragglers," Dino replied then stared at the distant look on Ravin's face. His expression obviously disturbed him, compelling him to attempt to control the situation. "This will all be over soon enough. You'll see. Carter and Anderson should have reached the neighboring town by now. I'm sure help will be along any minute. They'll probably run into Reed and Scott somewhere along the main road on their return, that way the authorities will know what they're dealing with."

"I wish I shared your optimism, Mayor," Ravin replied with little emotion and headed across the lobby toward the front desk.

✝

*G*emma sat on her guestroom bed in the white, plush signature hotel bathrobe. She hugged her knees to her chest and stared blankly at a speck of dirt on the carpet. There was an urgent pounding on the door. Gemma flinched with a startled gasp but didn't look away from the dirt on the carpet. The pounding continued for another few seconds then finally subsided, leaving her in silence. She lifted her head and looked at the bolted door. Gemma slowly and hesitantly crawled from the bed and tiptoed across the carpet to the door, being careful to avoid the speck of dirt. She hesitated before the door and finally summoned enough courage to look through the peek hole. When she saw no one at the door, she sighed with relief and ran her trembling fingers through her mussed hair. She seemed to relax and turned. Her attention again focused on the speck of dirt. She eyed the spot suspiciously then headed for the bathroom.

The white marble and tile bathroom was almost too cheerful considering her current mood. She ran hot bathwater to fill the tub and headed back into the bedroom. She again looked at the door. Everything was quiet. Gemma slowly rounded the speck of dirt on the floor, approached the bolted door, hesitated, and again looked through the peek hole. She saw someone's eye staring back at her. Gemma jumped back while screaming. She stared at the door in silence while attempting to control her rapid breathing. She slowly and nervously returned to the peek hole, again looking through it. There was no one there--just empty hall. She groaned softly and turned.

The speck of dirt was no longer on the floor. She stared at the clean carpet a moment, appeared suspicious, and then returned to the bathroom where her tub was filling. She shut off the water then looked in the steamy mirror at her reflection. She nervously ran her fingers through her hair in a half-hearted attempt to fix it. She frowned, giving up, and turned toward the tub while untying her robe. The tub was filled with bloody water! Gemma jumped back with a horrified look in her eyes while staring at the gruesome sight.

†

*T*he large lounge was furnished in early Victorian with rich colors of mauve and gold in detailed cheery wood. The massive ceiling to floor windows overlooked the pool and golf course. Despite the brilliant sunshine filling the room, none of the ten townsfolk within the lounge seemed to notice. Ravin paced the lounge with a bottle of water in his hand. Some of the others intensely watched him pace as if it was a sporting event. Sonya and Felicia flipped through old magazines and looked completely bored. It was so quiet that the ticking of the old grandfather clock sounded like a freight train. Thundering footfalls from padded feet were heard within the hallway and closed in on the lounge alerting everyone. Gemma ran into the lounge, clutching the plush bathrobe closed against her naked body beneath, and ran to Ravin. She didn't stop in time to keep from colliding with him. He caught her arms to keep her from falling. The look in her eyes was wild and frightened. She was out of breath and trembling despite his firm grip on her arms.

"There's blood--"

"Blood?" Ravin demanded. "Where?"

Felicia and Sonya hurried toward them while the other seven stared at the hysterical woman with horror in their eyes. Gemma was nearly down to tears and gripped Ravin's jacket lapels with clenched fists. She no longer cared about her nearly open bathrobe, despite her exposed cleavage. She possibly didn't even notice her robe was partially open.

"I went to take a bath, and the tub was filled with blood," she said as the words spilled from her mouth in a wave of emotion and near hysterics.

"Which room?" he asked.

"110," she gasped and gave a slight nod over her shoulder while clinging to him.

Ravin loosened her grip on his jacket and hurried her from the room while remaining on her heels. Felicia and Sonya hurried after them, leaving the others baffled and worried. Gemma ran through the main corridor in her bare feet and entered the first floor guest wing corridor. She paused just outside the closed guestroom door and panted while trembling. Her death grip on the plush robe wasn't enough to keep her cleavage contained, although no one seemed to notice. Ravin stepped in front of the door, removed his master keycard, and ran it through the reader. He pushed open the door, hesitated only a moment, and then stepped inside. All three women followed him at a safe distance. Ravin approached the open bathroom door and peered inside. Gemma was nearly down to tears while watching Ravin in the bathroom doorway. Sonya and Felicia each clung to Gemma's arms, possibly for their own comfort. Ravin hesitantly looked across the nearly spotless bathroom. The tub was filled with water, but there wasn't any blood within it. He was bewildered and looked back at Gemma.

"There's no blood," he informed her in an almost scolding manner.

"The tub was filled with blood!" Gemma suddenly cried out with unfounded rage.

Ravin approached, took her by the shoulders, and gently guided her into the bathroom. Gemma fought against his grip, now facing him, and became hysterical while nearly spilling out of her plush robe.

"No, no. I don't want to go in there!" she screamed in terror while clutching at his jacket.

Ravin steadily guided Gemma into the bathroom despite her hysterics. She reluctantly looked into the tub while frantically clutching at Ravin as if attempting to crawl inside his clothing with him. She stared at the tub filled with clean water and appeared alarmed.

"There was blood," she gasped and looked back into Ravin's eyes only inches from hers.

As she clutched and clawed at his clothing, Ravin attempted to keep her robe closed and conceal her naked body beneath, which he finally noticed. She was completely unaware that she nearly flashed him and was determined to climb his body.

"I'm telling you the truth!"

"I know what you think you saw," he informed her while pulling her robe closed over her cleavage to no avail. "But there's nothing there."

She clutched and clawed at him, defeating his attempt. Each time his hand brushed against her chest, he became even more flustered.

"I'm not crazy," she cried out in a tone that suggested she was.

Ravin looked across the bedroom at Sonya and Felicia, who just watched while he struggled to keep Gemma robed. "A little help?"

Both women snapped out of their trances and approached to assist him with the squirming Gemma. He released her robe, pulled her hands free from his jacket, and bolted away from the hysterical woman. Sonya and Felicia attempted to keep her calm and grabbed her discarded clothing from the bed. Ravin slipped from the guestroom looking frazzled and possibly embarrassed from his eyeful of the nearly naked woman.

Chapter Four

*R*avin, looking exhausted, walked along the grand hallway toward the lounge with the three women in tow. Gemma was now changed back into her clothing and seemed unusually quiet. She avoided looking at the other three with an expression that was difficult to read. It was hard to tell if she was embarrassed, frightened, or angry. Ravin suddenly stopped the three women not far from the lounge, sending alarm through them.

"Did you hear that?" Ravin asked in a whisper while looking around.

The three women looked around with shared paranoia.

"Hear what?" Gemma suddenly gasped with the fear evident in her eyes as she wrung her hands together and frantically looked around. She was just waiting for something to send her into panic-induced hysteria.

"I heard something too," Sonya said and looked around with concern as well.

"I didn't hear anything," Felicia remarked but looked as well.

Ravin hurried down the hallway. The women followed from a safe distance with some apprehension. A tall, lanky man wearing tattered clothing covered in blood dragged an ax behind him as he disappeared into the game room. Ravin stared with a look of alarm then ran after him. All three women hurried after him. Ravin entered and looked around the deserted game room filled with table and electronic games. The three women entered the room behind him and scanned the empty room. Gemma was frightened into a state near hysterics.

"Did you see him?" Ravin suddenly demanded and sharply looked back at the three women. "Some creepy guy covered in blood and dragging an ax."

"Well, he's not here now," Felicia said with some reluctance to believe Ravin's story.

Gemma latched onto Ravin and clung to his arm. "Can I go to my room now? I really want to go to my room," she stammered while nearly down to tears.

"It was a ghost. It had to be," Ravin boldly announced and seemed unaware of Gemma clinging to him and clutching his clothing as her fear escalated.

"I really want to go to my room now," Gemma said while sobbing. She had his jacket sleeve crinkled in her clenched fists and practically pulled it off him.

Ravin continued to scan the room and was still unaware of Gemma's death grip on his jacket.

"There's no one here and there are no ghosts," Felicia firmly insisted. "I don't know what you saw, Mr. Waverly, but you didn't see any ghosts."

Ravin sharply glared at her and was about to lash out when realization appeared to dawn on him. His expression slowly dropped, and he uncertainly shook his head. "Ghosts?" he announced with surprise and chuckled in his throat. "What's wrong with me? I know better." He sank into thought for a long moment then looked at the women with concern. "We've all been drinking the tap water. There must be something in the water that's causing hallucinations. It's the only reasonable explanation."

Gemma continued to clutch and claw at Ravin's jacket sleeve. Ravin nervously pulled Gemma into his arms and against him without a second thought. She immediately clung to him while shivering and held back her sobs. She was still attempting to crawl into his clothing with him, now clutching at his shirt. He didn't seem to notice or simply didn't care. If it hadn't been for the frightened expression on her face, her actions could almost have been mistaken for sexual aggression.

"We need to just slow down and remain calm," Ravin informed them then looked at Gemma in his arms. He now seemed aware of her traveling hands but didn't think much of it. He raised her chin and forced her to meet this gaze. "It's not real. None of it's real," he said firmly. "Just try to relax. We're going to be fine if we keep our heads."

She stared into his eyes, and for a moment, she didn't seem concerned. She seemed content just to stare into his blue eyes. She no longer clawed at his clothes and instead firmly ran her hands along his chest and shoulders in a more sensual manner. Sonya and Felicia immediately noticed Gemma's odd behavior. They exchanged bewildered glances. It was possibly more disturbing that Ravin didn't seem to notice. A woman's hysterical screams shattered the silence. Gemma screamed in response and nearly climbed Ravin's body. Her once caressing hands now clawed mercilessly at his shirt and ripped a button off without realizing it. Her nails dug into his shirt and scratched his chest beneath leaving blood trails through his shirt. He reacted with a gasp and clutched her clawing fingernails with less of a reaction than expected.

"Something's happened!" Gemma cried out in horror. "Oh, God! Something's happened!"

Ravin pried Gemma from his body while trying to keep her from clawing him and looked at the other women. Both were equally alarmed now.

"We need to check on the others," he quickly announced with concern.

Ravin ran from the game room with the three women on his heels. He hurried along the connecting hall, skidded just before the lounge doorway, and ran into the lounge with Felicia and Sonya just behind him. All three immediately stopped. There was blood everywhere! The seven people who had remained in the lounge were slumped in their chairs. All seven had slits across their wrists and blood from the deep gashes freely dripped onto the floor. Darlene, who stood just inside the lounge, stared with frozen horror at the seven dead people. She barely looked at Ravin and the two women standing only a few feet from her. She was most likely in shock.

"What happened?" Ravin demanded, jolting her from her trance like state.

She looked at him with surprise and her mouth hanging open. "I--I don't know," Darlene said while vigorously shaking her head and attempted to control her trembling body. It was little use. "I found them like this."

Dino, Tyson, and Cody hurried into the lounge just behind them, stopped abruptly, and shared the same look of horror at the gruesome sight.

"Holy shit!" Cody cried out and took a step back. "What the hell happened?"

Ravin apprehensively walked across the lounge and eyed the seven dead people slumped in their chairs. A straightedge razor lie on the floor in a pool of blood near one of the bodies. He stared at the razorblade then looked at the bodies with deep slits across their left wrists and blood on their right fingertips.

"They all have blood on their hands from the razor," Ravin announced softly and shook his head with disbelief. The horror was evident in his eyes. "These people killed themselves one after another."

The look of horror on the others' faces was beyond description as they stared at him.

"Are you sure?" Felicia gasped. She seemed unable to grasp the concept of a mass suicide.

"That's messed up," Tyson cried out and shared her disbelief. A concerned look crossed his face. "Do you suppose we were also poisoned? Not enough to kill us but enough to make us crazy?"

Sonya appeared alarmed and looked at her brother. Ravin shook his head in response.

"No, we weren't poisoned, but I think we may have been drugged," Ravin informed them then collected his wits. He took a deep breath and slowly released it. He attempted to stay calm. "We need to resist the urge to panic. We need to remain calm." Ravin looked back at the others and was about to speak when he looked around the room. His brows suddenly knitted into concern. "Where's Gemma?" he demanded.

The others looked around the room as well. Gemma wasn't with them.

"She was right behind us," Felicia insisted.

"I haven't seen her," Tyson replied.

Ravin became alarmed, bolted from the room, and ran into the grand hallway. He frantically darted in and out of nearby rooms while searching for Gemma. "Gemma! Gemma!" he cried out with the appearance of a madman.

The others entered the grand hallway and watched Ravin running in and out of rooms while screaming for Gemma. They shared the same look of disbelief.

"So much for remaining calm," Dino muttered. He shut the lounge doors behind them, tied them together with some rope, and then looked at the others. "His recent paranoid outburst aside, Ravin is right," Dino informed them. "We need to stay calm. We should split up into groups, find the others, and meet back in the lobby. No one goes anywhere alone."

"Ravin thinks the well water may have been tampered with," Felicia informed Dino.

"Figures," Dino scoffed. "When I suggested it, he thought I was being paranoid."

Tyson was surprised by the conversation but nodded in agreement. "Okay, then we'll only drink bottled water for now," he announced firmly. "There are cases of the stuff in the kitchen."

"That's a good idea," Dino replied while patting his nephew on the shoulder. "Let's find the others before something else happens." He casually pointed down the hall. "Tyson, you take your sister and Felicia. Check the kitchen, indoor pool, spa, and gym. Cody, Darlene, and I will take the front of the hotel. We'll meet back in the lobby in one hour."

Tyson gathered Sonya and Felicia and herded them down the hall in the direction of the spa and pool area. Dino indicated for Cody and Darlene to head in the opposite direction.

Chapter Five

$\mathcal{F}$elicia, Sonya, and Tyson entered the massive enclosed indoor pool room surrounded with walls of glass. The amazing pool area was expensive and lavishly constructed with a separate hot tub, tile flooring, and an indoor waterfall circulating from the pool. The impressive waterfall ran red with blood-tinged water. All three suddenly stopped and stared at the once elegant indoor pool. Twelve dead bodies floated face down within the water, now tinged red with blood. Despite the tinged water concealing their bodies, their gapping, slashed wrists were visibly and grotesquely noticeable. All three stared at the fully dressed dead men and women within the pool with shared looks of horror.

"What the hell is going on around here?" Tyson suddenly cried out, unable to tear his eyes away from the gruesome sight in the pool before him.

"I think I'd like to go to my room now too," Felicia said softly while clinging to her chilled shoulders.

"Look," Sonya gasped with alarm. "Their wrists have been slashed just like the others."

"I'm not buying this mass suicide bullshit," Tyson snarled with increasing agitation. "Ain't nothing can make a bunch of people spontaneously kill themselves like that."

"Maybe Ravin was right," Sonya gasped as her eyes widened while staring at her brother. "Maybe the hotel is haunted."

"You're all crazy," Tyson scoffed while shaking his head. "We need to be looking for this crazed killer and stop him."

"If it's all the same," Felicia announced, "I think I'd rather lock myself in my room until help arrives. I'm not interested in this whole safety in numbers business. It didn't help any of the dead people we've found so far."

"I'm all for hiding in my room too," Sonya announced and pleaded with her eyes to her brother.

He reluctantly groaned. "Fine, but first we need to find any remaining survivors," Tyson said sternly then sneered at them with disapproval. "Then you girls can hide under your beds."

Sonya glared at him with annoyance. "Do you have to be such a prick?"

"Under the circumstances? Yes," he snarled.

✝

*D*ino, Cody, and Darlene entered the dismal sunroom with its wall of glass and lavish hanging plants. Beyond the massive wall of windows, the outside sky had turned dark and stormy. The room was filled with wicker furniture and there appeared to be only one man remaining within the seemingly empty room. The older townsman in his fifties swung a baseball bat repeatedly to the floor just beyond the wicker sofa while grunting with each blow. All three watched him and looked puzzled. Blood flew from the bat as he pulled back for another swing and spattered the wall of glass behind him. The glass was covered with dripping blood. Dino held the others back and nervously moved closer to the older man. He stared at the bat dripping with blood. As Dino rounded the wicker sofa, he saw the man beating the bat into an unrecognizable woman lying in a bloody heap on the floor. She was completely smashed and broken from over one hundred strikes. She resembled roadkill exploded by a semi-truck. Another man lie not far away in the same condition. Cody uncertainly approached his brother, stood alongside him, and stared at the gruesome sight. The older man stopped beating the dead woman and looked at Cody and Dino.

"I saw them. I saw the demons," the man cried out with a look of fear and possible desperation in his eyes. "They were taking over their bodies." As he stared at both men, his eyes suddenly widened with alarm. "Look out!"

The older man pushed Dino aside and swung the bat at Cody's head. Cody gasped with alarm and dodged the baseball bat, which struck the wicker sofa. Dino swiftly punched the man in the throat, instantly dropping him to his knees. The man wheezed and attempted to catch his breath. Cody stared at the discarded, blood-soaked baseball bat then looked at his brother. Dino stared at the wheezing man on his knees and showed no remorse.

"What do we do with him?" Cody gasped.

"There are some tools in the workshop," Dino replied. "We'll rig a bolt outside one of the guestroom doors and lock him inside until help arrives."

"This is insane," Darlene gasped from across the room as she stared at the barely recognizable remains on the sunroom floor. "We need to get out of here. We need to hike to the nearest town for help before we end up killing one another."

"Anderson and Carter--" Dino began, but he was interrupted by Darlene.

"Anderson and Carter never made it," she launched back. "Help would have been here by now."

"We sent Reed and Scott," Dino stated more firmly. "They're former military men. They're survivors. They'll come back with help. We should stay put."

"She's right," Cody reluctantly informed his brother. "We need to send others for help. This is unreal. We're not going to survive much longer at this rate."

Dino stared at his brother and frowned. "Fine, we'll send out a couple more scouts," he replied then pointed a warning finger at Cody. "Just remember, I was opposed to sending more men. We don't know what's happening in here much less out there."

"Fine," Cody groaned, "you've been duly noted as the voice of reasoning. Now let's get more scouts out there and bring back some real help."

"I should go," Darlene announced.

Both men looked at her and appeared skeptical.

"Why you?" Dino demanded. "Do you have some special ops training I don't know about?"

"No," she replied, "but my friend has a horse on the other side of town--"

"Sorry, Darlene," Dino announced while shaking his head, "you're staying here. We don't know what's out there, if anything. I'm not willing to risk your life."

She glared at him, folded her arms across her chest, and frowned disapprovingly.

He raised his brows in question. "What? I'm sexist?" Dino demanded.

"You said it, I didn't," she snapped in response.

"If it keeps you alive, fine, I'm sexist," he replied then glared at Cody. "Let's find the others."

✝

*G*emma sat alone in the corner of the wine cellar with her knees to her chest and her head buried into her knees. She seemed almost sedate and made no sounds. Someone was heard entering the wine cellar, alerting her. Gemma nervously looked up and glanced across the row of wine racks as she was approached. She suddenly gasped and quickly sprang to her feet while staring with wide eyes. The terror suddenly shown in her eyes as she flattened herself against the wine rack. Gemma screamed hysterically while clutching the rack behind her.

Chapter Six

One day later. The night sky was black from the violent storm as rain poured down upon the deserted, backcountry road not far from Fox Ridge Village. It had rained for nearly twenty-four hours and most of the roadways were flooded. Water cascaded in small waterfalls through washed out shoulders along the road. The wind whipped and rain seemingly fell sideways as it blew across the backroad in sheets of water. A newer car was stranded in the flooded roadway nearly three feet deep with the water almost halfway up the car door. The car's flashing hazard lights alerted an approaching car to the severity of the flooded roadway ahead. A BMW pulled up and stopped a safe distance behind the stranded car. The driver of the BMW, Roger, got out of his car, opened an umbrella, and hurried toward the stranded car before him. The driver of the stranded car opened his window and looked at Roger as he approached. Roger quickly assessed the situation even though the verdict was pretty obvious. The car wasn't going anywhere.

"You're not getting out of that tonight," Roger shouted above the pouring rain. "Come on! We'll give you a lift to the nearest town!"

The couple in their fifties, Milton and Peggy, got out of their marooned car and waded through the three-foot high water toward Roger. Roger gave his umbrella to the already soaked woman. Milton and Peggy were dressed lavishly from an extravagant evening out, although their clothes were already soaked from the pouring rain and the murky standing water. Roger hurried them to his awaiting car. Having given up his umbrella, he too was now soaked. Another car, a Corolla, pulled up behind Roger's car. As the couple climbed into the back of his car, Roger hurried to the car behind his. The window rolled down to reveal a younger couple, Shane and Leslie. They looked concerned about what may have happened on the road ahead.

"The road is flooded," Roger said above the pouring rain. "GPS says there's a side road to a small town called Fox Ridge Village. Hopefully, there's access to another major road through there. GPS is spotty in these parts."

"Thanks," Shane said to the soaking wet man. "We'll follow you."

Roger hurried back to his car. Another car, a Lexus, approached behind the Corolla and slowed to join the parade of stopped cars. Roger jumped into the driver's seat of his BMW. His wife, Rose, sat in the passenger seat, stared at him, and appeared concerned over his soaked condition.

"My wife and I appreciate this," Milton said while leaning forward from the backseat. "I couldn't get any reception on my cell phone."

"Cell phones are sketchy at best on good days in these backwoods," Roger informed him and was almost humored despite his soaked condition. His wet clothes were almost certainly ruining the expensive leather seats. "You won't get anything in a mess like this. I'm lucky my GPS is working as poorly as it is. I have no idea where we turn once we reach town."

Rose eyed her soaked husband and cleverly raised her brow in suggestion. "We could always stop and ask directions."

Roger snorted a laugh and put the car into gear. "Silly girl," he scoffed while casting a sly grin at her. "Real men don't ask for directions. Real men have GPS."

"GPS is taking you down a backroad to some hick town in the middle of nowhere," she replied casually. "What will you do then?"

Roger shrugged. "Just drive around aimlessly until GPS picks up a signal."

"Oh, my God," Peggy softly chimed in from the back, "they're us twenty years ago."

Rose partially turned in her seat and grinned at Peggy in the backseat. At least the women were in good spirits under the circumstances.

The BMW turned onto the backroad to the right with the Corolla following. The Lexus obediently followed them. The driver of the Lexus, an attractive, young woman in her mid-twenties, Devon Pennington, followed the barely visible Corolla taillights. Devon wore a stunning, short black dress. She was returning home from a work related fundraiser party in a neighboring city. It was a miserable night to be out, and she regretted having gone to the party even more now. The party was a bust, and she couldn't imagine things getting much worse. Now that she followed the two strange cars along a dark, backroad in the pouring rain, she stood corrected. Things had gotten worse. She just hoped the leader knew where he was going, because she certainly had no idea where the backroad led. Headlights from an SUV shone through her rearview mirror as it gained on her. She eyed her rearview mirror and stared at the closeness of the vehicle behind her. She couldn't believe the nerve he had to drive so close to her back end.

"In a hurry, are we?" Devon scoffed to the headlights behind her. "Jerkoff--"

Devon hated when other driver's rode her ass. It wasn't as if she could pull over and get out of his way. Even if she could, she wouldn't have. She didn't believe rude drivers should be rewarded. To her, they were no different from children throwing a temper tantrum to get their way. Despite the pouring rain, heavy wind, and barely visible road, the SUV remained close to her bumper. Her horrible evening wasn't getting any better. The party was boring and did little more than leave her exhausted and driving some dark backroad in the pouring rain. Now she had an impatient driver crawling up her rear end. She again glanced at the SUV through her rearview mirror. With the mood she was in, she seriously wanted to slam on the brakes and let him ram into the back of her car. She desperately wanted to lash out at someone, and the SUV driver fit the bill. She finally tossed the idea from her head. He wasn't worth the effort. Devon sometimes wished she was more confrontational, but her rational side almost always took over. She clutched the steering wheel and cursed the SUV driver through the rearview mirror instead. Sadly, it wasn't nearly as satisfying as she had hoped.

The driver of the SUV, Novak Delano, was a lanky, well-dressed man in his mid-thirties. The man riding alongside him in the passenger seat was Vander Hawk, a ruggedly handsome man in his early thirties. Novak appeared irritated while keeping his attention on the taillights of the Lexus directly in front of him. He shook his head with annoyance and indicated the car to his friend.

"You know, if people are afraid to drive, they shouldn't be on the road," Novak said sternly. "Did you notice? It's always the women too."

Vander casually glanced at the man in the driver's seat and showed little reaction. "Damned right," Vander huffed under his breath. "They need to leave speeding through flooded roadways during a massive storm to the real men."

Novak glared at his passenger. Vander caught his stare then grinned teasingly.

"You know, I never liked you," Novak remarked dryly.

"The feeling's mutual," Vander said with a chuckle.

All four cars drove along the darkened road no more than thirty miles an hour in the pouring rain. A small, luxury party bus now trailed behind the SUV while maintaining a safe distance. The luxury party bus was lavish with bench style, leather seats and a massive bar. Loud dance music blared while twelve drunken, well-dressed men cheered as two scantily dressed women danced seductively around the stripper poles inside the bus. The professionally dressed, female driver in her late twenties glanced through the rearview mirror at the drunken, rowdy men. Monica Burke shook her head and rolled her eyes at the spectacle.

"I so didn't sign up for this," Monica muttered. "Damned well better tip good."

The BMW picked up speed and drove through the partially flooded roadway ahead. The water parted in tall waves on either side of the car. The Corolla drove through the parted water directly behind the BMW. The Lexus followed through, maintaining a safe distance. As the SUV closed in, the Lexus moved faster through the flooded roadway.

Within the BMW, Roger and Rose squinted through the heavy rain and thrashing windshield wipers at the tiny, blinking light up ahead.

"What's that light?" Rose asked her husband.

Milton and Peggy were equally curious and strained to see from the backseat. Roger's eyes suddenly widen in horror as he gasped and slammed on the brakes. Rose screamed simultaneously and clutched the dashboard. The BMW slid along the wet road toward the sawhorse with the 'bridge out' sign on it. The car struck the crude blockade and drove nose first into the ravine where the Fox Ridge Village covered bridge once stood. It crashed to the bottom nearly fifteen feet down, smashing the front end on impact. The

Corolla's brakes screeched as it slid toward the ravine and struck the partially exposed tail of the BMW, smashing it against the remains of the bridge. The Lexus veered to the side while sliding and nearly spun completely around. The Lexus avoided the Corolla but slammed into a tree with a thunderous crack, striking the rear passenger side. The SUV skidded wildly on the slick road, sideswiped the back of the Corolla, and spun directly into the back fender of the Lexus. It jolted the Lexus away from the tree and tossed it nearly horizontal with the SUV. The party bus veered to the right to avoid the Corolla on the left, skidded wildly on the wet road, and slammed into a tree to the right. Steam poured from the massive wreckage of mangled cars in the pouring rain.

Chapter Seven

*T*he party bus was eerily silent as interior lights dimly lit the passenger space of the bus. Strobe lights flashed but the music no longer played. Monica was slumped in the driver's seat over the steering wheel as blood ran down her left temple. She slowly woke, momentarily disoriented, and then looked behind her to the interior of the bus. The twelve men and two women were scattered haphazard throughout the back. Arms and legs pointed in every direction from the sudden impact and lack of seat restraints. For a moment, it seemed as if no one moved and their conditions were unknown. A few moans finally broke the silence and the passengers started moving and collecting themselves. Despite her bleeding head, Monica wasted little time reaching under the driver's seat for the first aid kit and crawled toward her injured passengers.

Within the Lexus, Devon was reclined unconscious against her seat with blood running down her left temple. The sound of shattering glass woke her as the safety glass showered her body. She looked to her left and saw a man unlocking her door through the broken window. Vander, soaking wet and his shirt tinged with blood, pulled open the door. He leaned over her and touched her face while checking her bleeding temple. In her disorientation, she stared at the soaked man hoovering over her and wondered who this handsome man was.

"Hey, are you okay?" Vander asked gently.

Reality returned to her, and she realized she was still in her car, although she couldn't remember what she had been doing prior to the moment she saw the handsome man alongside her. Nothing seemed to make any sense. Had she been driving?

"What happened?" Devon said weakly.

The sound of her voice was almost foreign to her, and she had a difficult time catching her breath. She then realized the seatbelt must have knocked the wind out of her. It remained tight against her chest and nearly suffocated her.

"Vander!" Novak was heard calling through the rain. "Over here!"

Vander remained in the doorway hovering over Devon while attempting to remain calm. "We've been in an accident," he gently informed her. "You may have a concussion, but you're going to be okay. I need you to stay here and try to remain still. I have to check on the other cars. I'll be right back."

Vander hurried through the rain toward the Corolla. Novak stood next to the passenger side of the car. Leslie had injuries to her head and held her arm. Shane also sustained multiple injuries, but he seemed less inclined to move.

"How badly are you hurt?" Novak asked the couple through the open doorway.

As Vander approached Novak alongside the Corolla, he glanced toward the front of the car. The bumper of the BMW stuck partially out of the ravine. It was the only part of the car that remained visible and with the taillights out, it was easily missed.

"Oh, shit--" Vander gasped.

Novak quickly straightened and looked toward the remains of the BMW. The horror was evident on his face. Novak looked back inside the car to Shane and Leslie.

"Can you move?" Novak asked with more urgency.

"Yeah, I think--" Shane began.

Novak pointed to the bus and didn't wait for Shane to finish speaking. "See if that bus has a CB radio and call for help," he announced firmly. "We'll use that as a mobile medical center until help arrives."

Shane uncertainly nodded. Novak joined Vander in the pouring rain just before the ravine. Both stared down the ditch at the BMW standing vertically on its nose. The roof of the car was seemingly crushed against the remains of the bridge. Devon slowly approached them while clutching her head and stared in horror at the car. Her hand fell from her temple.

"We have to get down there and see how badly they're hurt," Vander said to his friend. "Give me a hand."

Devon stared at the car below with her mouth hanging open and appeared horrified. "They're dead--" she gasped softly.

Vander suddenly looked at Devon with surprise and straightened. "What?"

"They're dead; all four of them," Devon said softly without taking her eyes off the car.

Vander and Novak exchanged looks. Vander looked back at Devon and placed his hands on her arms, forcing her to meet his gaze. She stared at him in the pouring rain.

"You've suffered a concussion," Vander informed her. "You need to join the others in that bus."

Devon looked past him and again stared at the car below. She wasn't about to tell them what she saw. It was something she learned never to discuss. The ghostly images of Roger, Rose, Milton, and Peggy clung to one another in the ravine while staring at the vertical, smashed car. The four ghostly men and women looked up at Devon. She stared back at them with sympathy. Their spirits shot upward in a flash of light. Devon shut her eyes and turned her head as the rain continued to drench her.

Novak helped Vander climb down into the ravine alongside the car. Vander looked at the bloodied driver's side window, hesitated only briefly, and firmly yanked on the door until it opened. Roger's skull was seemingly split open on the side where he hit the driver's window. His seatbelt held him firmly against the seat despite his vertical incline. Rose was impaled by a plank from the remains of the old covered bridge. The plank had shattered the windshield and gone straight through her chest. Milton and Peggy both lie bent and broken against the backs of the front seats, having not worn seatbelts. Neither moved and both had their eyes open while seemingly staring at nothing. Their heads were twisted severely to match the rest of their broken bodies. Vander shut his eyes, groaned softly, and then climbed back up the ravine. Novak took his hand and helped pull him the rest of the way. Vander slowly shook his head, indicating his findings. Both men looked at Devon in silent question.

†

$\mathcal{O}$ne hour later. Everyone remained quietly seated within the party bus while tending to their injuries with the limited supplies from Monica's medical kit. Shane constructed a makeshift sling with his leather belt to stabilize his wife's broken arm. Shane frowned while staring at his wife's bleeding temple.

"I wish I'd listened to you and just stayed home tonight," Shane said softly.

Leslie managed a tiny smile and gently touched his face. "Not exactly the romantic evening you'd planned," she replied. "But I appreciate the effort."

Shane snorted a soft laugh and kissed her warmly on the lips. "Always the optimist."

Monica tended to head injuries and taped some of the more serious cuts together. Vander again checked his cell phone and shook his head with disgust. Several other injured passengers attempted to get signals with their cell phones as well, but it was no use. No one was getting a signal in the remote backwoods in the middle of nowhere.

"We're cut off from civilization," Vander announced with disgust to no one in particular. "We need to hike to that town and find some help."

"That town is at least a mile from here past what was supposed to be a bridge," Shane sternly informed him. "My wife has a broken arm. She can't tackle that ravine and make that journey." He indicated the other injured passengers within the bus. "With all these injuries, not many of us could make that."

"Novak and I will go," Vander informed Shane and the others within the bus. "We'll find whatever help we can."

"I'm going with you," Monica announced without hesitation and stood.

Novak looked at Monica several feet away from him. "You should probably stay here," he informed her. "It could be dangerous."

She glared at him through narrow, squinted eyes. "I served two tours in Iraq," Monica scoffed with obvious annoyance by his comment. "I think I can handle a mile hike through the mud and rain. I'm also an EMT. If I can find some decent medical supplies, I can patch up these people and stitch their wounds." Monica folded her arms across her chest and sneered at him. "But if you'd prefer to stand around and argue about my qualifications, I can do that too."

Novak didn't know what to say, indicated by his blank stare and his mouth hanging open. Monica accepted his silence as 'no' to a confrontation. She headed for the front of the bus and routed through the glove compartment. Two men who had been traveling together on the party bus, Harris Fitch and Trent Lawler, stood and approached Novak and Vander.

"We're coming with you," Harris announced. "We're okay to travel."

"Those are our friends. Some have been hurt pretty badly," Trent said. "We want to do our part to help them."

"Our friend's getting married next weekend," Harris announced. "If we don't bring him back in one piece tonight, his fiancée will kill us."

"Fine," Vander reluctantly replied. "The five of us will hike to that town for help and medical supplies. The rest of you need to wait here."

Vander, Novak, Harris, and Trent walked toward the front of the bus where Monica waited with a baton-style flashlight in her hand. Devon watched them head for the front door. Something told her she needed to go. She needed to leave the bus and go with them to Fox Ridge Village, and she needed to go now. She quickly sprang to her feet and joined them at the front of the bus.

"I want to go too," Devon announced.

All five eyed Devon in her short, black dress and heels. Novak chuckled in response. Devon immediately felt her cheeks redden from Novak's chastising chuckle.

"No offense," Vander announced firmly, "but you're not exactly dressed for the occasion. You won't get far in that dress and you'll be lucky to make it ten feet in those heels. You'd better sit this one out."

Devon frowned. She didn't know why she had to go, but she knew when she got those feeling, she needed to listen to them. This feeling was urgent. She couldn't possibly explain it to them, and they'd never understand. Most times, she didn't understand. Monica grabbed a duffel bag from the nearby compartment, opened it, and tossed a leather jacket and sneakers to Devon.

"Welcome to the boy's club," Monica announced.

Devon eyed Monica with surprise. She wasted little time slipping into the jacket and shoes before anyone attempted to stop her from tagging along. She wasn't about to question Monica's motive, but she was pretty sure it was meant as a gesture to piss off Vander. Vander appeared stunned by Monica's actions and glared his disapproval at her.

Monica glared back at Vander, folded her arms across her chest, and raised a cocky brow. "Is there a problem?"

Vander looked at Novak for a comment or reaction. Novak hid his smile but offered neither. Although Devon didn't know Monica, she already knew all she needed to know about her. She wasn't the type to take crap from anyone, and Devon was convinced she had the means to back it up. That being said, Devon was just happy she was on her side.

Chapter Eight

*T*he small town of Fox Ridge Village was unusually dark and consisted of only a few dozen homes and businesses. Many had been boarded up with 'for sale' or 'for rent' signs in the windows, adding to the eeriness of the darkened, deserted town. The six crash survivors walked along the dark street while being drenched by the heavy rain. As they looked around the abandoned town, none felt at ease toward their steadily worsening situation. Devon didn't understand why she felt the urgency to leave the warm dry bus to hike out to a ghost town. It made no sense. Usually when she felt a strong need to do something, it was for a good reason. That wasn't the case tonight. Now she was wet, cold, and confused. At least she wasn't alone. Her travel companions were equally confused, although for completely different reasons.

"It's almost as if everyone packed up and left in a hurry," Novak said as he looked around. Several parked cars caught his attention. He became tense and suspicious. "Except they forgot to take their cars."

"Anyone else getting a bad feeling?" Harris muttered while attempting to keep the rain from running down his jacket, although he was already soaked.

Devon wanted to respond but thought better of it. Her bad feeling started before they even left the bus, but she couldn't tell them that. No one responded to Harris' comment, but they were obviously all thinking the same thing.

"The registration stickers on the cars are current," Vander casually replied while eying the license plates on several cars parked near them.

"Where do you suppose they went?" Trent asked while studying several boarded buildings.

The others felt compelled to look at the current stickers on the cars as well. It was unsettling seeing so many cars seemingly abandoned, but if they weren't abandoned, what happened to the residents? Devon felt chilled from more than just her soaked clothing against her skin. If the others shared her concern, they were able to hide it better than she did. She looked toward the woods and froze with fear. Tiny, dancing lights flickered deep within the woods. Their likeness to fireflies made them seem almost harmless, but Devon knew it wasn't fireflies. The flickering lights were an ominous pale blue and their appearance concerned Devon. Monica eyed Devon, noted her strange look, and then glanced in the direction she stared. Beyond the woods, the lights from the hotel on the hillside were visible.

"There are lights coming from that big building," Monica informed them while pointing beyond the woods.

The others instinctively looked and immediately appeared surprised by what they saw. For a luxury resort, from their perspective, it looked more like a castle from a horror movie beckoning them closer.

"There are lights on," Trent remarked, "so someone's home."

"Big building nothing," Harris gasped then suddenly grinned. "That's a hotel."

Novak groaned then relaxed. "That explains it," he remarked and snorted a soft laugh. "This is a summer town. No one lives here during off-season. We'll find help at the hotel. There are lights on. Someone's obviously there."

"That's another mile through the woods," Monica bluntly informed them. "The injured need medical attention now--not tomorrow."

"There's no one here," Harris remarked. "How are we supposed--?"

Monica casually pointed to a small building with a sign that read, 'veterinarian'. "I'm getting some medical supplies and heading back to the bus," she informed them.

"There's no one in that office," Trent replied. "Looks like it's been abandoned for some time."

She glared at him, lacking patience. "I wasn't looking for an invitation," Monica replied and flipped her flashlight, clutching it like a baton. "I have a key."

There was an odd silence among them as everyone except Devon stared at Monica and her weapon of a flashlight.

"Okay," Vander gently replied with a sigh.

Novak looked at Vander and appeared surprised. "Okay?" he suddenly announced. "You're okay with her breaking into someone's business?"

"Those people on the bus need medical attention, and she's their best hope at the moment," Vander replied then looked at Monica. "You take the medical supplies back to the bus. We'll hike to the hotel and see if we can get help."

Trent assessed their situation then turned to Monica. "I'll help you with the supplies."

"Fine, just keep up," she remarked and briskly crossed the street toward the vet's office.

Trent hurried after Monica through the pouring rain. Vander, Novak, and Harris headed toward a path that seemingly led to the hotel beyond the forest. Devon stood in the middle of the street with the rain drenching her and continued to stare at the flickering lights within the woods. Panic filled her as she searched for an explanation to what she saw. Something nagged her to continue onward, but another part of her screamed for her to return to the bus. Her conflicted emotions were eating away at her. The three men realized she didn't follow. They stopped and looked back at her.

"Hey, are you coming with us or heading back to the bus?" Novak called back to her.

Devon didn't respond. Actually, she hadn't heard him. Novak took two quick steps back to her.

"Hey," he announced more firmly.

Devon snapped out of her trance-like state and looked at Novak through the pouring rain.

"Are you coming with us or going back to the bus?" he again asked.

Her instincts told her to go to the hotel. Despite her wanting to return to the bus, she hurried to join Novak and the other men. She wasn't sure if she'd made the right decision, but something compelled her to press onward. Her instincts weren't always right, but she needed to see what the lights meant. For some strange reason, it was important.

Chapter Nine

It had taken nearly an hour for Monica and Trent to gather supplies from the vet's office and hike back to the scene of the crash. Both were completely soaked and trudged with exhaustion the last few feet to the unusually quiet bus. Monica pulled open the door and entered the bus carrying the soaking wet backpack filled with supplies. Trent followed just behind her looking worn and exhausted. Monica stopped abruptly, allowing Trent to collide with her from behind. He was about to protest her sudden stop when he saw what startled her. The fourteen men and women remaining on the bus were slumped in their seats or lying on the floor. Blood soaked their clothing, surrounded their bodies, and spattered the seats and walls. Both were horrified and momentarily rendered speechless at the gruesome sight.

"What the fuck!" Monica finally cried out.

Trent clutched her arm firmly and pulled on her while nervously looking around. "We need to get the hell out of here!"

Monica pulled her arm free from his hand, dropped the backpack, and approached one of the dead women, who lie face down on the aisle in a pool of blood. She slowly rolled her over. It was Leslie. Her throat had been slashed so deeply, she was nearly decapitated. Trent paced the front of the bus and appeared ready to jump out of his skin. It was possible whoever killed them wasn't far away. Trent could barely look at the gruesome sight and obviously felt concerned by Monica's need to have a closer look.

"We have to get out of here," Trent gasped while running his fingers through his wet hair more than a dozen times. For as nervous as he was, Monica was twice as collected.

"Hold up--"

Trent spun toward her with concern in his terrified eyes. "Whoever did this might come back," he announced with panic in his voice then looked around. "Maybe they never even left. We don't want to be here if they return."

Monica scanned the rest of the dead men and women from her crouched position near Leslie. Shane sat slouched on the bench seat not far from her in the same condition. Each man and woman had deep gashes along their throats but no other marks. None had any blood on their hands, indicating they hadn't even clutched their throats as they bled to death. Monica was obviously disturbed while studying the scene.

"There aren't any signs of a struggle," she gasped softly and became further alarmed by her findings, "or that they even tried to escape their attacker. It's almost as if they just sat there and allowed someone to kill them one by one."

Trent was about ready to explode and her fairly creepy remarks weren't easing his stressful condition. "Monica, we need to go-- now!"

Monica straightened, grabbed the backpack, and quickly followed Trent from the bus. As they stepped off the bus, Monica stopped and scanned the crash site as it lightly rained on them. Trent looked back at her and was concerned by her curiosity. He was ready to bolt, quickly losing patients.

"Let's go," he cried out softly.

Monica ignored him and continued to scan the area while clinging to her flashlight. The expression on her face was disturbing. Trent was about to yell at her, but she held her hand up to silence him before he could speak. Trent's eyes widened with horror as he quickly scanned the area, attempting to see what had caught her attention. He took two quick steps toward her.

"What is it?" he whispered.

"We're being watched," she softly replied without tearing her eyes away from the area behind the bus. "There's someone or something out there." Monica indicated the area beyond the party bus with a slight movement of her head, alarming Trent. "Over there--by the rear exit of the bus."

Trent stared at the back of the party bus and trembled. "Do we run?" he asked softly.

"No," she replied.

"No?"

"We're going to walk toward the ravine and head for that town," she informed him while keeping her eyes fixed on the back of the bus. We don't know what's out there. If it's a wild animal, it'll chase us. If we walk away, it might leave us alone."

"And if it's the crazed psycho killer who killed all my friends?" he softly demanded.

"We'll see him coming and lock ourselves in the car stuck in the ditch," she replied without taking her eyes off the rear of the bus. "Start walking."

Trent nervously started walking toward the ravine. Monica clung to her baton-style flashlight and backed up behind him, keeping watch behind the bus and the surrounding area. Trent attempted to climb down the partially muddy ravine. He suddenly tumbled to the bottom with a startled scream. Monica rolled her eyes. There was loud movement within the woods.

She groaned softly. "Oh, fuck--"

Monica quickly turned, jumped down into the ravine, and landed gracefully near Trent. As she pulled him to his feet, something moved within the woods. Trent took off across the ravine and scrambled up the other side. Monica watched him run like a frightened rabbit, cursed under her breath, and ran after him.

†

𝒰ander, Novak, Harris, and Devon walked along the darkened path within the woods in the direction of the hotel. Judging by the worn path, it was traveled frequently by those living in town who worked at the hotel. The rain had tapered to a lingering shower, but the cool, night air chilled the weary, wet travelers. The lights from the hotel were obscured by the woods, but they were certain the path led to the hotel. Devon lagged behind while staring at the dancing lights, which were now just up ahead. As they approached, it became obvious that the dancing lights were ghostly spirits. The others were unaware of what Devon was witnessing. She lived alone in her own private hell. She slowed and watched the spirits as they aimlessly floated around the woods. Several spirits looked at her with the same look of confusion. Devon stopped and stared at the spirits. Seeing them collected was odd in itself, but their confused state and location seemingly in the middle of nowhere troubled her. Vander returned to her and stared at the blank look on her face with concern.

"Are you okay?" Vander asked.

Devon couldn't tear her eyes away from the spirits just ahead. She uncertainly shook her head and attempted to warm her soaked body by rubbing her shoulders through the leather jacket. "Something's wrong," she said softly.

"You probably have a concussion," Vander gently informed her. "You should have waited in the bus. It's not a good idea for you to be out here in your condition."

Vander was well-meaning, most people usually were, but they didn't understand. Most didn't even want to know the things she knew. Normal people couldn't handle the reality of it.

"I'm fine," she gently informed him rather than explain.

He stared at her a moment then groaned softly. "Why are women always so stubborn?" he asked while shaking his head. "Come on; let's get you to the hotel."

Vander attempted to guide her along the path where Harris and Novak now stood waiting for them. Devon reluctantly walked with Vander but looked back at the spirits. Every restless spirit seemed to stop and now stared at her with the same blank, confused expression. Their direct contact with her was alarming. It was something she rarely experienced. With so many of them now staring at her, she felt unusually insecure. Something was terribly wrong. She quickly took Vander's hand for added security. He glanced at her with some surprise, offered a reassuring smile, and led her along the path. She wished she could explain it to him, to make him understand, but even those closest to her rarely believed what she told them she saw. If she was lucky, they just laughed at her. Most times, she was looked at like some crazy person, so she learned not to talk about it. It was for the best. She again looked back. The spirits watched her in silence.

Devon felt her entire body shudder in response. Vander must have felt it and squeezed her hand in response. She felt compelled to look at him as he smiled back at her. For a brief moment, she felt a terrible feeling of dread sweep over her. The last time she'd felt something that chilling was moments before a man accidentally stepped out in front of a city bus. Did she just have some sort of half-assed premonition? Was Vander destined to die? She clung to his arm with her free hand, shut her eyes, and wished the terrible feelings away. When she opened her eyes, she realized Vander stared at her as they walked. He offered an oddly tender smile that chased her fears away.

✝

*M*onica and Trent hurried along the dark, backroad toward town in the drizzling rain. Trent looked around nervously, watching what was behind him more than what was in front. Whatever had been lurking around the crash site didn't seem to be following them, or at least they hadn't heard or seen anything. Something moved within the woods to the right and caught Trent's attention. He suddenly stopped and stared at the woods to get a better sense of what was out there. Monica grabbed Trent by the arm, startling him, and roughly pulled him into the woods to the left. The forest was the quicker way to town, and the trees would also provide some shelter in the event of an attack. As she moved faster, so did Trent. She hurried through the woods with Trent on her heels. Whatever it was he'd heard, she'd heard it too, and it was now following them. Both instinctively looked back. Within the darkness, something fairly large darted through the shadows.

"It's back there!" Trent cried out while attempting to keep up with the agile woman.

"Come on!" She didn't stop or bother looking back at him, but instead remained focused on where she was going.

"It's gaining on us," he yelled to her while paying more attention to the woods than where he was running.

"Run, you idiot!"

Monica now ran through the woods with Trent attempting to keep up with her. She skillfully maneuvered around trees, over roots, and past rocks that were barely visible in the dark woods. Trent looked back several times, causing him to trip over roots and rocks. The creature appeared to be closing in on him, and Trent's fear showed. He stumbled over an exposed tree root and fell to the ground with a yell. Monica slid to a stop, spun around, and looked back at him where he lie on the ground. Trent slipped within some mud by the tree while attempting to scramble to his feet. Monica ran back to help him. The creature was some sort of animal, which was now partially visible within the shadows of the trees as it rapidly closed in on them. Monica tossed the backpack to the ground, raised her flashlight in a deadly fashion, and prepared to fight off the predator. As the creature leaped from the woods, Trent screamed. Monica cried out and swung the flashlight.

Chapter Ten

The four explorers from Vander's group reached the open, resort grounds several acres before the massive hotel a little after midnight. Devon paused a moment, awestruck by the impressiveness of the hotel but was immediately pulled along by Vander's hand securely clutching hers. She was already having bad feelings about the hotel, but she didn't know how to tell the three men about it without sounding like a crazy woman. She could almost hear them laughing at her now as others in the past had laughed. She hoped her instincts were wrong this time, as they sometimes were, but the spirits within the woods told a different story. There was something serious and frightening happening, and she knew the small, abandoned village had something to do with it. The chill running down her spine as they approached the massive resort told her the disturbing occurrence had spilled over to the hotel as well. They approached the covered driveway just before the large, double doors. Novak attempted to open the doors, but they were locked. He knocked using the large knockers. There didn't seem to be any other means of contacting someone within the hotel, and the question as to if anyone would even hear them knocking was clearly on each of their minds. As Devon stared at the intimidating doors towering above her, she knew something sinister awaited them just inside.

As Novak assessed the massive, locked doors, he muttered to his companions, "I don't know about the rest of you, but I'm missing Monica."

"I don't think her flashlight would get us in through this door. There has to be other doors," Vander said with a defeated sigh. He looked around the exterior of the massive hotel. "We certainly can't stay out here all night."

"Can't we just break down the door?" Harris demanded with a tone of impatience.

Vander and Novak slowly turned their heads and glared at Harris with shared disbelief to his ill-conceived comment.

Novak extended his hand toward the massive, thick doors and grinned. "Be my guest."

Devon snorted a soft laugh. "You'd need a tank to get through those doors," she remarked while rubbing her soaked, cold shoulders through Monica's drenched leather jacket.

"We'll walk the perimeter and find a more vulnerable entrance," Vander informed them. "If we have to, we'll break down a smaller door."

The main door clicked as it was unlocked. All four looked toward the thick doors as one of them opened, allowing light to spill out onto them and the covered driveway. Ravin stood in the doorway in his expensive suit and stared at them with a strange look of bewilderment. He had a noticeable bruise on his jaw and three fresh scratches along his neck. Novak and Vander eyed him suspiciously after seeing the scratches. Devon was more curious than suspicious.

"Where in the world did you come from?" Ravin suddenly asked.

"There's been an accident," Novak informed him while maintaining a look of distrust.

"Around here?" Ravin asked with surprise and looked beyond the driveway as if expecting to see wrecked vehicles on the property. His actions were bizarre.

"No, just off the main road," Vander replied while studying the man in the doorway. "The bridge was out."

"Oh, that," Ravin said casually while placing a hand in his pocket. His look turned serious. "You must have walked a long way."

"No kidding," Harris mumbled. "Do you think we can use your phone and call for help? People have been injured. My friends are out there."

Ravin stared at them a moment as if not understanding the question. "Oh, I'm afraid that's quite impossible," he informed them. "The phones haven't worked for days. Perhaps you should come inside and warm by the fire."

All four exchanged looks then hesitantly entered the hotel past Ravin. Devon hesitated just outside the door while clinging to her shoulders. She stared blankly through the open doorway. Something was very wrong, indicated by the hairs on the back of her neck standing on end. A cold shiver ran up her spine, reinforcing what the little hairs were expressing. Ravin stared back at her in silent question. She didn't even look at him. He was about to speak when Vander stepped outside, took her by the arm, and pulled her into the hotel while keeping her close to his side. Ravin watched them enter, appeared curious, and then followed them inside. He casually closed the door behind them.

✝

*R*avin passed fresh towels to the four, soaking wet guests now standing by the fire in the lobby's massive, stone fireplace. The impressive lobby was stylishly rustic with exposed beams and expensive southwestern furnishings and decorations. Despite the hotel's beauty and grandeur, Devon felt uneasy but couldn't understand what was causing those feelings. There were times that she wished her gift came with a handbook. As she looked at her travel companions, she noticed they shared some of her concerns but obviously not the same ones. Novak and Vander seemed particularly suspicious of Ravin. She wondered if they had some divine inspiration when it came to reading people, or if they were just naturally suspicious of everyone. Her ability to read people was part of her gift she just recently started to understand and develop. Novak and Vander had an air of confidence about them. It wasn't just a macho thing but something far greater. It was that odd feeling she'd get while passing the courthouse. She suspected it was because of all the overinflated egos in such a confined space.

Their suspicions of Ravin weren't unfounded, in her opinion. Ravin's expression and demeanor seemed oddly off, but she couldn't put a finger on it. She felt as if he was hiding some dark secret, and each time she looked at the scratches on his neck, it sent chills down her damp spine. Any normal person would find the scratches concerning, naturally, but they screamed to Devon. She sensed the violence and trauma that placed them there, but she didn't feel anything aggressive or dangerous about the man sporting them. He was almost too calm both outwardly and from the vibes she was receiving. The chills she received from just being inside the hotel suggested something traumatic. It seemed inconceivable that the calm, neatly dressed man sitting before them wasn't aware of whatever had happened within the walls. Ravin sat on the arm of one of the sofas with little expression while studying his guests.

"Sounds like you've had a harrowing night," Ravin said with almost no emotion. "I wish I could tell you something that might cheer you up, but I'm afraid things are about to get worse for you."

Devon felt another shiver down her spine. The temptation to run from the hotel was strong, but she fought her secondary instinct and instead listened to what her gift was telling her. She needed to stay. For whatever reason, she wasn't supposed to leave. The others just stared at Ravin with puzzled looks.

"Don't tell me there's no way to reach help, because that's the last thing I want to hear," Harris announced.

"Oh, if it was only that," Ravin replied dryly. "The last thing you want to hear is far worse."

Devon felt her entire body twitch to his chilling words. She couldn't read his emotions, but whatever he was hiding was rapidly surfacing. That she was fearful but not of him made little sense.

"What happened?" she asked timidly.

He glanced at her with the most serious look and slowly shook his head. "Honestly, I have no fucking clue."

Novak leaned closer to Vander and muttered, "He's definitely on something." He indicated Ravin with a tiny nod. "Do you want to take this one?"

Vander tossed his towel onto a nearby chair, removed his badge from his pocket, and flashed it at Ravin.

"I'm Special Agent Vander Hawk, FBI, and this is my partner, Special Agent Novak Delano," Vander announced in a stern, authoritative voice.

Novak flashed a smile along with his badge. Harris and Devon looked at both men with surprise, although it did explain the vibes she was getting from them.

"You can either start cooperating," Vander informed him, "or I'm arresting you for substance abuse and failure to assist a federal agent in an emergency."

"Substance abuse?" Ravin asked with genuine surprise while anxiously standing. "I'm not on anything, I assure you, but I am glad you're here." He suddenly seemed more enthusiastic and actually appeared almost relieved. "There's something I think you should see."

Ravin hurried into the grand hallway with all four following. He paused before the dining room and unlocked the doors. As he opened the door, Vander and Novak looked inside. Both men stared with shared looks of horror at the gruesome scene.

Harris peered over their shoulder and jumped back with alarm. "Oh, shit!"

The day old remains of those poisoned remained within the dining room where they had fallen. Nothing had been disturbed, not even the food on the tables. Novak suddenly grabbed Ravin, slammed him face first against the nearby wall, and removed his handcuffs.

"You're under arrest!" Novak cried out.

Ravin barely reacted to Novak's outburst and physical contact. His look remained callous and unchanged. "I didn't do this," he casually replied. "The hotel's haunted."

Novak handcuffed Ravin, roughly turned him around, and pushed his back against the wall. "Nice try."

Devon couldn't look away from the massacre within the dining room. As she stepped into the doorway, Vander immediately stopped her. She stared, as her mouth hung open, at the nearly seventy spirits floating around the dining room circling the dead bodies. A few looked at her with the same confused expression as the spirits within the woods. Every spirit suddenly stopped and stared at her. Devon rubbed her chilled arms and stared back at them. Why were they staring at her like that? It was unlike anything she'd ever encountered before. A tidal wave of horrifying images flashed through her mind of the men and women vomiting and grasping the tables while attempting to stand. She watched them collapse while gasping for air and clutching their stomachs. Frightened screams echoed throughout the room as others watched helplessly or attempted to comfort them. Devon took a deep, shaken breath, and suddenly grabbed Vander's arm for support. He pulled her away from the doorway to keep her from seeing the grisly sight. She leaned against the wall and panted while holding her head. An enormous headache struck her and pounded within her skull. She'd never felt such intense pain before, but then again, she'd never witnessed a scene of mass death before.

"I didn't kill them or the others," Ravin said calmly.

Vander released Devon and approached Novak. Both federal agents exchanged horrified looks to his comment about 'others' then glared at Ravin. Neither seemed to know how to react.

"Others?" Vander demanded in disbelief. "There are more dead people?"

He nodded. "We've all seen the ghosts," Ravin informed him. "They're causing some sort of mass paranoia among the others. I'm not entirely sure why I haven't been affected."

Devon slowly raised her head without releasing it and looked at Ravin with surprise to his ghost comment. If her head hadn't been pounding as it was, there was a chance she'd be able to understand what happened better.

"Where are these other live people?" Novak demanded, although his tough guy attitude had been replaced with something resembling alarm.

"It's one o'clock in the morning," Ravin replied matter-of-fact. "The others are attempting to get some sleep. I could wake them, if you insist."

Novak sneered at him and raised a cocky brow. "Yeah, I think we're going to insist." He forced Ravin away from the dining room.

Chapter Eleven

*T*he elevator doors opened on the fourth floor to reveal Ravin with his hands cuffed behind his back and Novak standing alongside him. He pushed Ravin into the corridor. Vander, Harris, and Devon followed Novak and his prisoner. The fourth floor corridor was wide with multi-colored carpeting and tasteful decorations that screamed glamour and glitz. The resort was obviously a wealthy man's rustic retreat. They headed to the end of the hall and paused before the corner suite.

"Would you mind knocking for me? I'm a little tied up right now," Ravin casually said while indicating his cuffed wrists behind him.

Novak groaned with limited patience and knocked on the door. There was no response. Novak waited only a moment before pounding on the door.

"That's not such a good idea," Ravin announced and fidgeted for the first time. He attempted a tiny, nervous smile. "My, uh, girlfriend is a little out of *sorts*."

"This is your room?" Vander demanded and quickly became annoyed. "Where's the key?"

"Oh, that's not wise, Special Agent Hawk," Ravin said as his eyes widened. "Even I wouldn't go in there without her permission. She's not exactly *herself* right now."

Novak slammed Ravin face first into the wall and searched his pockets for the key. Devon and Harris jumped with surprise by his burst of hostility. Ravin didn't even react. Novak removed the card key from Ravin's jacket pocket, flashed it with a smirk, and unlocked the door. It made a metallic chirping as it electronically unlocked. Novak opened the door and looked around the suite. There wasn't anyone home. Vander pushed Ravin inside. The condition of the once lavish suite was frightening. Several busted items lie scattered about the room as well as empty bottles of wine, bottles of water, and large cans of half-eaten fruit. Novak walked across the room while Vander remained with Ravin just inside the doorway. Devon and Harris peered into the room just over Vander's shoulder.

Ravin casually called out, "Darling, we have guests."

Novak slowly approached the open doorway to the darkened bedroom. Nothing moved and there was no response. The silence frightened Devon, and even though he wouldn't admit it, she could sense Novak was frightened too. Gemma lunged from the bedroom and tackled Novak to the floor. She landed on top of him, straddling his waist, and punched him in the face while crying out like a wild animal. Vander grabbed Gemma around the waist from behind and hoisted her off Novak. She kicked and screamed wildly with her arms and legs thrashing against him. She was nearly impossible to hold. Vander tossed her onto the sofa. She bounced with a scream, leaped to her feet, and lunged for Vander. Vander swiftly caught her wrist, and in one fluid motion, twisted her arm behind her back. He pushed her face first against the nearby wall and held her immobile. Although not physically hurt, she appeared stunned by her confined position.

Ravin hadn't moved and showed no reaction to the attack or capture. "She's quite vigorous," he casually announced, surprising everyone.

Vander swiftly cuffed Gemma's wrists behind her back. His attention was immediately drawn to the bruises already on her wrists. He spun her to face him. Gemma threw her back against the wall and stared at Vander with fright.

"Who are you?" Gemma demanded with a gasp. She had the look of a wild woman with unkempt hair and oversized clothing that obviously belonged to a man.

"It's okay," Vander announced while attempting to sound calm and reassuring. "We're here to help you. You don't have to be afraid. It's going to be okay." He indicated Ravin across the room. "What's he done to you?"

Gemma was puzzled and looked at Ravin near the doorway. He smiled charmingly at her. She suddenly smiled with enthusiasm, completely reversing her earlier hostility.

"Hey, baby," she chirped.

Everyone exchanged bewildered looks. Obviously, something was wrong. Vander hesitantly removed Gemma's handcuffs. She gingerly rubbed her bruised wrists but didn't seem the least bit affected by any of what happened. It was almost as if she didn't even remember the last five minutes.

"Where did you get the bruises?" Vander asked her.

She stared at Vander with surprise then glanced at the bruises on her wrists. "It wasn't his fault," Gemma insisted while looking back at Vander. "I went a little crazy." She looked at Ravin and smiled apologetically.

"Just a few scratches, dear. I forgive you," Ravin gently informed her then looked at Vander. "I didn't mean to cause those bruises, but you saw her zesty exuberance."

She flashed her neatly trimmed, polished fingernails with great pride while grinning. "He gave me a manicure."

Harris stared at the scene with his mouth hanging open then turned slightly to Devon and muttered, "What the hell is going on here?"

Devon slowly shook her head while staring at Gemma. "I have no clue, but it's starting to freak me out a little."

"Is he holding you against your will?" Vander asked Gemma with a little more sympathy.

She appeared surprised by the question. "Who? Ravin?" Gemma suddenly asked. She looked back at Ravin, gave him a seductive once over, and smiled lustfully. "No, of course not. He's my little stud muffin." She blew Ravin a kiss from across the room and winked at him. She seductively ran her fingers along her cleavage in an attempt to arouse him.

Ravin grinned with a dreamy sigh and looked at Harris. "I'm her stud muffin--"

Harris and Devon exchanged looks but withheld comment.

"You're kidding, right?" Novak suddenly bellowed out with disbelief.

"Why is he handcuffed?" Gemma politely asked.

Vander seemed stunned by the question. "Because there are dozens of dead bodies littered across the dining room, and he makes a damned fine suspect."

She defiantly shook her head. "No, it wasn't him, it was the ghosts," Gemma announced with conviction and immediately turned fearful. "The ghosts poisoned them and made the others kill themselves. We didn't touch anything. We didn't want to--" She hesitated then glanced at Ravin with a curious tilt of her head. "What was it you said?"

"We didn't want to compromise any evidence," Ravin replied casually.

Gemma groaned lustfully. "He's *so* smart." Her look almost instantly turned serious. She frantically looked from Vander to Novak. "The others know what happened. You should talk to them. They'll tell you. They'll tell you it was the ghosts. You can't arrest Ravin. He didn't hurt anyone, I swear. He wouldn't." She suddenly turned paranoid and grabbed Vander's arm while pleading with her eyes. "I can't live without him. I'll die for sure. Don't take him away from me--please!"

"Okay, that's enough of 'psycho love story'," Novak snarled then glared at Ravin. "Wake the others. This entire situation is starting to creep me out."

"Tipped my 'creepy-o-meter' long before this," Harris muttered to Devon.

"Mine too," Devon replied in response. "And that's tough to do."

Chapter Twelve

$\mathcal{I}$t was a little before two o'clock in the morning by the time Ravin had gathered the remaining survivors in the lobby. Apart from Ravin and Gemma, Dino, Cody, Tyson, Sonya, Felicia, and Darlene were all that was left. Vander, Novak, Harris, and Devon again stood near the fireplace in their still soaked clothing. Devon was shivering partly from dampness but mostly due to their alarming situation. The remaining townsfolk shared Ravin's take on what happened within the hotel over the last forty-eight hours. Novak and Vander were less than convinced. Harris just stared without comment, but he obviously thought the same thing. They were all out of their minds! Devon couldn't get a read on any of the other survivors. It happened often while around groups of people. In this case, stress levels were alarmingly high, even among those in her group. General consensus told her they were telling the truth; or at least they believed they were telling the truth. Either way resulted in the same disturbing outcome. Gemma stayed close to Ravin. Felicia, on the other hand, seemed to be working the room and was nearly oblivious to the conversation. She stopped and flirted with Dino.

"Seriously, you're all sticking with the ghost story?" Novak demanded and appeared less than impressed.

"We know what we saw," Dino informed them. He wasn't pleased with Felicia's hands caressing his shoulders and aggressively forced her away from him. He maintained his serious attitude and kept his attention on the federal agents. "I'm the mayor for Christ's sake. I know how it sounds, but I wouldn't make this up." He attempted to collect himself and drew a deep, shaken breath. "Unfortunately, you'll see for yourself soon enough. It's been quiet the last few hours. Too quiet, if you know what I mean."

Dino's cold rejection didn't even faze Felicia. She moved on to Tyson, who attempted to ignore her advances.

"We all saw them over the past twenty-four hours," Sonya said with some insecurity. "You wouldn't believe the hell we've been put through."

"One guy went completely mad and took a baseball bat to a few of the others," Darlene explained. "We saw him do it. He said they were possessed. The ghosts made him do it. Those were his words, Agent Delano."

"Every time someone leaves, they end up dead," Tyson informed them. "Leaving isn't an option. We have to wait for help to arrive. No offense, but we need *real* help."

"Most of us haven't slept in two days," Cody remarked then took a large swallow of scotch. "We're about ready to fall over from exhaustion."

Harris looked at Vander with concern and shook his head with conviction. "We need to get to the bus and warn the others. Ghosts or not, something killed those people."

"You can't go back out there--not in the dark," Ravin informed them with a look of concern. "You'll never make it past the woods. There's something out there, and you won't see it before it sees you. You'll end up like the others."

"Your ghosts don't scare us, Ravin," Vander remarked. "We've been through the woods. How do you think we got here in the first place?"

"It's not the ghosts you need to fear, Agent Hawk," Devon said almost too soft for him to hear. She couldn't sense whatever it was that had the entire group completely spooked and on edge, but she knew there was something evil within the hotel and surrounding the resort grounds.

Vander glanced at Devon alongside him and attempted to understand her comment. Her expression, although grave, offered him nothing. He then looked at Novak.

"We'll wait until daylight," Vander informed Novak. "Monica said she'd take care of the injured people on the bus." He glanced at the others seated within the lobby. They were generally relieved that the four weren't going back out into the woods tonight. "Is there anything safe to drink?"

"Wine and bottled water," Cody informed him. "I also found a couple of bottles of the hard stuff, if you'd prefer."

"I think we'll pass on the alcohol," Vander replied then indicated Cody's glass. "You may want to take it easy on the hard stuff yourself."

"Perhaps you'd like some dry things to wear," Ravin announced and cast a look at Devon as she shivered. "We have some waiter's uniforms cleaned and pressed from last season. If you'd like, I could get you some rooms, so you can clean up a little and maybe get a little sleep."

Once Tyson finally brushed off Felicia, she made her way closer to the damp, weary travelers and watched them intensely with lust in her eyes.

"I'm sure you're exhausted from your ordeal," Ravin said sympathetically.

"Yeah, a little," Vander replied but lacked enthusiasm considering their situation. "We'd appreciate some dry things and a place to rest."

"How many rooms?" Ravin asked then wagged his finger with a lustful smile between Harris and Devon.

Harris eyed Devon and grinned his approval. Devon glared back at him, successfully wiping the smirk from his face.

Felicia smiled lustfully and clung to Vander's arm, startling him. "There's room in my guestroom for one more," she cooed softly.

He stared at her a moment with surprise then gently pulled his arm from her clinging hands. The other three from his group were equally surprised at her forwardness.

Vander looked back at Ravin. "No one should be alone in their own room," he announced. "Give us two connecting rooms. We'll work it out between us."

Devon eyed Vander with surprise. What was he suggesting? If he was trying to be funny, she didn't appreciate it.

He caught her look and chuckled softly. "Hey, you wanted to join the boy's club," Vander teased.

Felicia's disappointment quickly faded, and she linked onto Novak's arm instead. He just stared at her with his mouth hanging open. She grinned sweetly.

"What about you?" she said seductively.

Novak wriggled out of her grip as well. "I'm on duty," he replied while studying her. Despite not knowing the woman, her behavior seemed off.

She looked at Harris and raised her brows suggestively in silent question. Harris grinned. Before he could speak, he caught Vander's stern glare. Harris gently cleared his throat and politely waved his regrets.

†

*R*avin led the four cold, damp newcomers along the second floor hallway toward their guestrooms. Vander stopped before one of the rooms that displayed a crudely installed slide bolt lock outside the door.

"What's with this?" Vander asked.

The others stopped. Ravin approached and stared at the slide bolt outside the door.

"Oh, that," he announced. "We locked our baseball bat wielding friend in there for safekeeping."

"When's the last time you checked on him?" Vander asked.

"Two days ago."

"Two days?" Novak demanded with surprise. "Didn't anyone bring him any food in two days?"

"I checked on him four hours after we'd locked him in there," Ravin informed them. "He slit his wrists in the bathtub. We left everything exactly the way it was for the arrival of the police."

Novak and Vander exchanged looks but neither man commented. Ravin led them further down the hall and paused before one of the rooms. Vander and Novak approached the room next door and let themselves in with a key card. Ravin unlocked the guestroom for Harris and Devon and opened the door. He held up the card between them and smiled slyly. His lustful expression was easy to read without psychic abilities. Ravin seemed to be in hormone overload, which was somehow unnatural from the vibe Devon was getting from him. She couldn't figure out exactly what was wrong with him, but she was almost positive he wasn't normally so uninhibited. Harris grinned and took the card without reservation. Devon sharply glared her disapproval. There was a loud thumping from the connecting door between the two rooms. Ravin casually unlocked and opened the connecting door to reveal Vander in the attached guestroom.

Vander glared at Harris and pointed a warning finger at him. "This door stays open."

Harris frowned, seemingly scolded. Ravin left the room without further comment, although he was heard softly snickering as he walked away. Once Vander disappeared into his shared room with Novak, Harris turned to Devon.

"Did you want the shower first?"

She fidgeted and attempted not to shiver. "I'll wait for the dry clothing," she replied. "You can go first."

A sly grin crossed his face. "Of course, we could take one together--"

Vander loudly cleared his throat from somewhere within the adjoining room, causing Harris to flinch.

"Or not," Harris replied then headed into the bathroom and closed the door behind him.

Devon rubbed her chilled, damp shoulders as she approached the window and looked outside into the darkness. Vander appeared in her room through the open, connecting doorway and studied her a moment while her back was turned.

"How's your head?" he asked gently.

She glanced back at him only briefly. "Okay, I suppose," Devon replied softly.

Vander casually leaned in the doorway and watched her. "I saw you at that charity benefit in the city earlier tonight."

She turned with surprise and looked at him. "Oh?" Devon didn't recall seeing him there and was actually surprised he'd seen her. "Not exactly the sort of event the FBI would crash," she teased while grinning.

"That's actually kind of funny, because we did crash it," Vander informed her and returned the playful smile. "We arrested a fugitive who was working there. It all went down quietly in the kitchen, so we wouldn't disturb the gala."

She laughed softly at his response. "Sounds like you had more fun than I did."

"That depends on your idea of fun," Vander teased. "Novak is a good dancer, but he never lets me lead."

Devon had to smile at his boyish charm. Vander wasn't nearly as serious when he wasn't around others or his partner. Perhaps it was just his tough guy act. She'd never actually met a federal agent, so she only knew what she saw on television. As she stared at him, her look turned serious. Their situation was no laughing matter, and she was still deeply disturbed by more than just the mass killings within the hotel. She was now convinced it was the restless, tortured spirits who commanded her presence, and things like that *never* happened to her.

"What do you think really happened here?" she asked almost timidly.

Vander straightened stiffly and shook his head. "I have a few theories I've been kicking around, but none seem to quite fit. We have a whole bunch of dead people and a handful of very frightened and confused people," he replied.

"But you agree that they're all a little *off*, right?" she asked gently.

"Off as in out of their minds?" Vander suddenly asked then laughed softly. "Yes, they're a little off. My first guess would be drugs, but I don't think they took any knowingly, and I certainly don't buy that mass suicide theory either."

"If you and Agent Delano are going to investigate further tonight, would you mind if I tagged along?" she asked then immediately fidgeted. "I promise not to touch anything."

He was surprised by the request. "Wouldn't you feel safer here with Harris?"

Devon's expression suddenly dropped at the suggestion. "You're kidding, right?"

He snorted a laugh then smiled gently. "He's harmless," Vander informed her. "Just a spoiled, rich boy used to getting his own way."

"If it's all the same, I'd feel safer with you," she informed him with little emotion.

Vander made an effort to conceal his pleased smile. He was obviously smitten by the comment and perhaps read a little too much into it. He sent a strong sexual vibe, which she easily detected, even with her limited psychic abilities.

"How can I argue with that?" he replied while grinning.

That the vibe he transmitted diminished quickly from her senses told her he was merely entertaining a wayward thought, with which he had no intention to act. Devon actually had her own reasons for wanting to tag along, and it had nothing to do with Harris or feeling more secure around her new FBI friends. She wanted answers to her own questions; questions they didn't even know existed. She was already feeling overwhelmed with sensory overload, but she needed to be involved. Her concern for their safety was frightening, but if she didn't open her mind and let the spirits tap dance on her brain, she feared something bad would happen to the others. She feared it would be something she could have stopped or possibly given them warning. She felt an odd need to keep Vander safe, and she wasn't entirely certain why. As she secretly studied Vander, something stirred inside her. It wasn't simply some secret sexual desire she was feeling, although the thought had crossed her mind, especially after the vibe he'd unwittingly sent her way. Agent Hawk was undeniably a handsome man, but this was something different. Devon desperately prayed her abilities weren't expanding or sharpening. She didn't want or need to become a full-blown psychic. She didn't need any more images floating around in her mind than there already were. She studied his handsome features a moment longer. Still--?

Chapter Thirteen

*R*avin stood by the door to the indoor pool area and watched Vander and Novak, who stood several feet away from the in ground pool. It was three o'clock in the morning. Both federal agents stared at the grisly sight of a dozen bodies floating in the water. Between the floating bodies and the amount of spilled blood, the pool resembled a grotesque stew of the dead. Devon stood near Novak and Vander with a pen and notebook in her hand. All three were freshly showered and changed into black pants and white shirts, which were the hotel's borrowed wait staff uniforms. Both federal agents proudly displayed their shoulder holsters worn over their shirts. Devon watched the spirits aimlessly circling the pool while Vander visually examined the bodies. He had no clue as to what she was seeing just above him.

The feeling she got within the indoor pool area wasn't nearly as intense as what she had felt within the dining room. It possibly had to do with less spirits in a confined area. A few fleeting images of a razor blade slashing across wrists invaded her mind, but to her surprise, there was no fear among the dead. They had been relaxed at the time of death, but she didn't know how that was even possible. She wished she understood what it meant, but she didn't. How could there be no fear among those who died? Fear was a natural response no matter how they met their demise.

"Their left wrists were slashed," Vander remarked then indicated the straight razor within a pool of blood by the pool's edge. "It's safe to assume that's our weapon."

"That's the same way we found the bodies in the lounge," Ravin informed him while placing his hands in his pockets. "We were gone from the lounge less than an hour."

"No signs of struggle," Novak remarked while glancing over the bodies with an equally puzzled look. "No other injuries that I can tell. I don't get it."

"Even with hallucinogenic drugs, I don't see how this is possible," Vander pointed out.

"They were murdered?" Ravin suddenly asked while staring dumbfounded. "But you agreed they didn't struggle. You're suggesting they just allowed someone to slit their wrists."

Devon wondered the same thing. Although, it would explain the lack of fear among the spirits in the pool area. It had to be drugs. There was no indication from the spirits that they willingly took their own lives. Their confusion confirmed that much.

"We're back to drugs," Vander replied.

"That's a lot of people to drug at once," Novak said while sighing deeply. He didn't appear convinced it was possible either. "I don't know how it could have been done."

Devon stared at the spirits of the dead people as they floated above the water. The spirits were now staring at her. She attempted to read their expressions. It was almost as if they wanted to speak to her, but that would be impossible. She'd never spoken with any ghosts in the past. Of course, they never seemed inclined to talk to her either. She just assumed it wasn't possible. What if they could? She didn't even want to consider it. That would mean her psychic powers were growing, and she didn't want the responsibility that came along with it.

†

*D*evon sat on one of the oversized chairs within the lobby and watched Vander and Novak talking quietly across the room while sipping bottled water. It was nearly four o'clock in the morning and the others had already returned to their rooms in an attempt to sleep.

How they could sleep under the circumstance was a mystery to her. Ravin approached Devon and handed her a bottle of unopened water. She smiled her thanks and accepted the water. He sat on the arm of the sofa closest to her chair and studied her with great interest. Something about the way he stared at her peaked her curiosity. He was difficult to read. She desperately wanted to read something from him, but she couldn't sense anything.

"You saw something back there, didn't you?" Ravin asked while tilting his head.

She gave him a bewildered look. "What do you mean?" she suddenly asked. He couldn't have known what she saw, unless he really did see ghosts too.

"The way you looked at those scenes of horror. You weren't looking at the bodies," Ravin stated then appeared curious. "Did you see the ghosts too?"

An odd feeling swept over her. It was almost a feeling of relief. Finally, someone else saw what she saw. For the first time, she didn't feel so alone in her bizarre world. Devon drew a deep breath and slowly nodded. "Yes, I see ghosts," she said softly. "But if you see them, you must realize they're not responsible for any of this."

"I've seen them carrying bloody axes and bloody knives," Ravin informed her. "That's enough to confirm they're responsible, don't you think?"

"No one was killed with an ax or a knife," she said simply. Her heart suddenly sank. He didn't see ghosts, at least not real ones. She hadn't found a kindred spirit after all, and it saddened her. "Ghosts don't kill people, Ravin. The only ghosts I've seen are those who'd died." She shifted in her chair while studying his expression. She desperately wanted to share her gift with someone. Perhaps he wasn't like her, but he wasn't going to laugh at her either. Confiding in him wouldn't be such a bad thing, and she desperately needed to get it out. "I saw the look on their faces. They're confused. They don't understand what happened to them."

"You saw the faces of those who'd died?" Ravin asked with surprise. "I only saw horrible, evil faces. Unfamiliar faces," he informed her then shook his head. "Something's wrong with me. I'm in a fog. My memory is sketchy, and that's not like me. I've loved Gemma my whole life, but somehow it doesn't seem real. Like it's a lie."

"There's a good chance you and the others have been drugged," she replied. "Do you remember anything before you felt like you were in a fog?"

He considered the question and seemed to have difficulty remembering. "I, uh, remember doing inventory with Gemma." He grinned. "She told me I was sophisticated and intelligent." Ravin then drifted out momentarily and tensed. "After the killings, I remember finding her alone in the wine cellar. I tried to comfort her, but she was afraid of me. No, it was as if she was *terrified* of me. I remember holding her while she hit me." He stared off and appeared to realize something. "Gemma and I were never lovers. I'm her boss. Nothing more. Why did I think we were something more?"

Ravin was extremely confused and concerned. Devon could finally feel some emotion from him. He was conflicted as his true personality attempted to surface. He was sad and lonely. She waited with anticipation for him to continue, for the real Ravin to reveal himself. She wanted to understand him, and in order to do that, she needed to sense some emotion. Any emotion would do. Gemma stepped into the lobby, approached him from behind, and leaned over his shoulder while smiling lustfully.

"Baby, are you coming to bed?" Gemma cooed soft and seductively.

The sexual vibe Devon received from the two was staggering, and she had to block them out before erotic images flooded into her mind.

Ravin looked at Gemma and smiled affectionately. "Absolutely," he announced then looked at Devon while grinning. "If you'll excuse me, I'm wanted."

Just like that, reality vanished, and he was trapped back in whatever world he was living at the moment. Ravin jumped up, pulled Gemma into his arms, and kissed her warmly but passionately. Devon felt their lust with a flood of emotion. It was almost enough to cause her to squirm in her chair. Sexual desire between two people was always tough on Devon. She tended to feel dirty, as if she was invading their intimacy. If their passion was strong enough, it sometimes mentally pulled her in as an unwilling participant. She didn't need to see and, in some cases, feel a couple's passion. Gemma was heating up fast. Devon squirmed slightly and contemplated leaving the room before sexual images of them flooded into her mind. Ravin broke off the kiss, grinned boyishly, and led Gemma from the lobby. Devon was relieved Ravin retained some of his gentleman reserve and had enough sense to take their sexual antics to the privacy of his room. Devon shuttered off remnants of their passion, stood from her chair, and approached Vander and Novak across the room. Despite their exhaustion, both men watched the couple leave and shook their heads with disbelief.

"I don't get it," Novak muttered.

"They've definitely been drugged," Devon informed them and attempted to hold back her shiver. The couple's lust lingered within the lobby after they were gone. It was an aftershock Devon hadn't been prepared for.

"Did either say something important?" Vander asked while rubbing his tired eyes.

"Not exactly," she remarked. "Ravin had thirty seconds of lucid thoughts. He admitted that he only worked with Gemma, and she was never his girlfriend. A second later, he's back to being her little stud muffin."

"Well," Novak remarked while deviously raising his brows, "if you're going to go--"

Vander shot a disapproving glare at his partner, silencing him. He looked back at Devon. "This is all tied in with the murders somehow," Vander said as he struggled to keep his eyes open. "As soon as it's light, we need to get back to the bus. We'll see if any of the cars will run and drive for help. If not, we'll hike to the main road."

"So what do we do in the meantime?" she asked while watching both men struggle to stay awake. Her adrenaline rush kept her from feeling tired; she was actually surprised theirs didn't do the same for them. Perhaps they were used to death and killings, so they were able to adapt better than she was.

"Being exhausted isn't going to do us any good," Vander replied. "It'll be sunup soon. We get a couple of hours sleep and then head out after daybreak."

"Honestly, Agent Hawk, I'm not sure I want to close my eyes even for a second in this place," she informed him while insecurely rubbing her arms.

"Novak and I are right next door," Vander informed her. "Despite the popular opinion poll, our killer's not a ghost, so he's not getting into our rooms without our permission. You'll be safe, I promise."

"Yeah, you'll be perfectly safe," Novak replied firmly then muttered under his breath, "because I'm certainly not closing my eyes."

t

*D*evon entered her dimly lit guestroom only a few minutes later through the open, connecting door from Vander's bedroom. She stopped just inside the guestroom and was surprised to see Harris sitting up in bed. He appeared exhausted while resting his head against the headboard. He managed to look at her but seemed too tired to move or speak.

"I'm surprised you're awake," she said to him.

Vander poked his head through the connecting doorway, having heard her talking, and obviously wanted to make sure everything was okay. Harris attempted to focus on her, having trouble keeping his eyes open, and slowly shook his head.

"Every time I doze off, someone knocks on the door," Harris informed her. "I get up to look out, but there's no one there. It was starting to freak me out. I'm glad you guys came back when you did."

"Well, let them knock. You need some sleep," Vander said firmly while standing in the open, connecting doorway. "Once it's light enough to see in the woods, we're heading back to the bus. You have a few hours to get some sleep."

Harris groaned softly. "I was ready to leave ten minutes after we got here." He studied Vander in the doorway. "What's the verdict? Did you find your killer?"

"I don't even have a proper suspect list," Vander remarked. "With the body count as high as it is, there's no telling who's dead and who's missing."

"They'd sent several scouts out to get help from a neighboring town too," Devon remarked. "None returned. One of them could have backtracked and committed the killings. No one would ever know."

"This night just keeps getting better and better," Harris snorted and attempted a weary smile as he slipped beneath the covers. He nestled his pillow and closed his eyes. "Wake me when you're ready to leave."

Before either could even respond, Harris was already asleep. Devon glanced at Vander in the open doorway. He nodded, indicating her bed.

"You'd better get some sleep," Vander announced. "It's a long hike back to the crash site."

"What about their warning?" she asked gently. "Do you believe everyone who leaves never returns?"

"These people have been drugged," Vander informed her. "We can't believe anything they say at this point. Novak and I are both armed. The two of us can handle whatever comes along out there in the woods." He hesitated and drew a deep breath. "Although, with the mass murder here in the hotel, waiting until daylight was the smart move. There's no telling what's out there."

"What are your thoughts on that?"

Vander drew a deep breath and sighed softly. "Personally, I'm wishing I hadn't watched so many hillbilly horror movies."

Chapter Fourteen

*D*evon slept restlessly while fully dressed beneath the covers within her shared guestroom. Her chance for solid sleep was continually interrupted by images of the massacre on the first floor and ghostly images staring at her as if wanting something from her. It was a little after five o'clock in the morning when she felt a hand brushing the hair from her face. Devon suddenly woke with a soft gasp. Harris sat on the edge of her bed while smiling at her. Devon cried out and jumped up with alarm. Her heart was pounding so hard in her chest; she could barely catch her breath.

"What the hell are you doing?" she finally screamed at him after her breath returned.

"You were having a bad dream," Harris replied with little reaction to her outburst.

There was an urgent pounding on the connecting door, startling both. To Devon's surprise, the door was closed and apparently had been locked as well.

"Open this door!" Vander was heard yelling through the locked door as it vibrated with each thump.

Devon sprang out of the bed past Harris and hurried for the connecting door. Harris casually returned to his own bed as she unlocked the door. Vander and Novak bolted into the room with their guns drawn and looked from Devon to Harris.

"I heard screaming," Vander announced with hostility. "Why was the door closed and locked?"

"There was too much snoring coming from your room. I couldn't sleep, so I shut the door," Harris informed him as he sat innocently reclined on his bed. "Devon was having a bad dream, and I guess I startled her."

Devon folded her arms across her chest and glared at Harris through narrow eyes. "He was being perverted and creepy," she muttered.

Novak replaced his gun to his shoulder holster. The disgust was evident on his face. "I told you leaving them alone together was a bad idea," he muttered to Vander while wearily running his fingers through his mussed hair.

"Oh, come on. I didn't do anything," Harris protested while seemingly pouting.

"Uh, huh." Vander nodded Devon into his room. She walked past both federal agents without hesitation and entered the room next door.

Novak suddenly eyed Vander and raised his brow in question. "So who's sharing a bed with the girl, because I'm definitely not sharing a bed with you?" he announced.

"Oh, that's easy--"

Vander pushed Novak into Harris' room and locked the connecting door behind him. Novak stared at the closed door with surprise.

"Oh, that's just cold, man!"

†

*D*evon slept peacefully on the second bed within Vander's room. Her haunting, scattered dreams had subsided, allowing her finally to get some quality sleep. The curtains were suddenly pulled open and sunlight flooded the room. She groaned softly and buried her face into the pillow, attempting to hide from the sun. She didn't know what time it was, but she wasn't ready to face another morning.

"Ten more minutes, Dad," Devon muttered.

"Rise and shine," Vander announced then scoffed softly, "and don't call me dad."

Devon opened her eyes and saw Vander walk across the room toward the connecting door. Realization of last night's horror quickly returned. She groaned softly and sat up in the excessively comfortable bed. She had hoped it was all just a bad nightmare, but she wasn't that lucky. Vander opened the connecting door to the room next door. Harris slept soundly in his bed, but Novak was missing from his bed. Vander took two steps into Harris' room, looked in the bathroom, and then glanced back at Harris beneath the covers.

"Where's Novak?"

Harris slowly woke, groaned softly, and looked at Vander near his bed. "How the hell should I know?" he muttered then turned onto his side facing away from him.

"Get up," Vander ordered. "As soon as we find Novak, we're heading back to the bus."

"Or you can find Novak first and come back for me in an hour," Harris muttered.

"I can also drag your ass from that bed," Vander snorted while casually placing his hands on his hips.

Harris groaned softly with exhaustion and sat up in bed. "I'm up; I'm up."

Devon shuffled into Harris' room looking rumpled and exhausted. "What's going on?"

Vander approached Novak's bed and snatched his discarded shoulder holster. He frowned while looking at the gun still in the holster. "Novak went for a walk."

"I guess he couldn't sleep," Devon remarked and leaned against the wall near the bathroom.

"He wouldn't leave his weapon lying around like that," Vander remarked and appeared preoccupied with his friend's sudden disappearance. "Everyone get dressed--now." He returned to the connecting room.

Harris sat up on the bed and stared after Vander. "He's a regular ray of sunshine in the morning."

"We'd better do as he says," she remarked gently.

"Yeah," Harris remarked sternly, "or he might shoot us." He grinned despite being tired. "So I guess you didn't make his night, huh?"

"You're begging to be shot, aren't you?" Vander was heard calling out from next door.

†

$\mathcal{V}$ander, Harris, and Devon stepped out of the elevator together on the first floor and walked across the massive lobby. Ravin stood by one of the large lobby windows with his hands casually in his pockets while staring outside into the warm, sunny morning. He appeared preoccupied with whatever he was watching. Ravin's calm demeanor was a mystery to Devon. Despite everything happening around them, he somehow managed to keep calm and together. Perhaps it was a side effect of being drugged; or maybe it was just all the sexual antics between him and Gemma keeping him mellow.

"Have you seen Agent Delano?" Vander asked as they approached him.

Ravin continued to stare out the window with little emotion. "As a matter of fact, I have."

"Where is he?"

"Running around naked on the front lawn," Ravin casually replied and pointed out the window.

Vander looked outside, seemed horrified by what he saw, and then ran for the front door. Devon and Harris approached the large window alongside Ravin and looked outside as well. Both were stunned and stared with their mouths hanging open.

"Wow, look at Agent Delano go," Devon announced under her breath. "What the hell is he doing?"

"Looks like he sat on a nest of fire ants," Ravin casually replied with little reaction.

"There's something you don't see every day," Harris muttered in response and laughed lowly.

"Oh," Ravin said casually and pointed in the opposite direction, "here comes Agent Hawk."

Their heads turned in response.

"And there goes Agent Delano," Devon replied.

There was an odd moment of silence as all three watched out the window, their heads turning in time with the track and field event just outside.

"Think we should go out there and help catch him?" Harris finally asked.

"No," Ravin replied with little emotion. "This is far more entertaining."

All three suddenly cringed. Devon gasped with horror while placing her hand to her mouth. She lowered her hand and raised her brows.

"Nice tackle, Agent Hawk," Devon announced.

Harris cringed and placed his hand to his crotch. "Oh, that's gotta hurt!"

Chapter Fifteen

$\mathcal{D}$evon sat on the first bed in Vander's room while Harris leaned casually in the doorway with his arms folded across his chest. Both stared at the closed bathroom door and listened as Vander and Novak argued from within the confines of the bathroom. It was a loud and heated exchange. If the situation wasn't so serious, Devon would almost have found the exchange comical. There was a soft tap on the door before the electronic hum. Ravin entered the room with a neatly folded bundle of fresh clothing for Novak.

"I don't know where he lost his clothing, so I brought him a clean set," Ravin announced.

The arguing continued from the bathroom, catching Ravin's attention as well.

"You don't need to hover over me," Novak yelled from within the bathroom. "I can take a shower by myself!"

"I'm not leaving you out of my sight!" Vander yelled back. "Federal agents don't run around naked in public!"

"There were spiders crawling all over me! I freaked a little, okay?"

"Federal agents aren't afraid of spiders!"

The bathroom door was thrown open, startling Devon and Harris. Both pretended they hadn't been listening. Ravin didn't bother acting innocent. Vander poked his head out of the bathroom, grabbed the clothing from Ravin, and glared at all three.

"Show's over," Vander growled then disappeared into the bathroom and slammed the door.

The three exchanged looks.

"Anyone else find this morning's events a little strange?" Devon asked.

"Compared to what?" Ravin asked.

"Okay," she replied while groaning. "Perhaps not strange compared to the last few days you've had, but strange according to the standard norm."

"The sooner we get out of here the better," Harris remarked. "There's something in the water. There has to be."

"No one's been drinking the water," Ravin casually replied while giving Harris a serious look.

"I didn't mean that literally," Harris remarked.

Devon glanced at Harris. "You thought someone was knocking on the door half the night, and this morning, Agent Delano thinks there are spiders crawling all over him. That's pretty bizarre behavior, don't you think?"

"Are you saying I imagined someone knocking on the door?" Harris suddenly asked.

"Do you really believe there were spiders crawling on Agent Delano?" she asked while cleverly raising her brow in question.

Harris stared at her a moment and considered the comment. "You're right, that is bizarre."

"It's the ghosts," Ravin informed them then looked at Devon. "You said you saw them."

She stared at Ravin with a horrified look to his mentioning that in front of Harris.

Harris looked at Devon with surprise. "You've seen the ghosts?" he asked.

"Ghosts didn't kill those people," she insisted sternly. "Something's happening here and now it's affecting us as well."

"You know what," Harris suddenly announced while straightening in the doorway. "I'll meet you guys outside. I've had about enough of this place."

The bathroom door opened to reveal Vander as he stepped out. He glared at Harris and Devon. His patience had all but been exhausted. "We're leaving in five minutes."

†

$\mathcal{V}$ander and Novak stepped out of the elevator into the lobby and continued to argue softly about Novak's earlier streaking incident. Neither seemed willing to let it go, and Novak maintained his insistence about the spiders. Devon, Harris, and Ravin followed after them and were already bored with the conversation. Dino, Sonya, Tyson, and Darlene waited in the lobby and watched them approach. Dino wore his usual tough guy expression and practically blocked their path to the main doors.

"You're not seriously going out there, are you?" Dino asked firmly, masking his concern.

"We need to return to the bus. There are injured people out there," Vander informed him and appeared annoyed by Dino's lack of compassion. "It wouldn't be a bad idea if some of you came along to assist."

"I'll go with you," Darlene said with some reluctance. "I have some first aid training. Maybe I can help."

"I'll go along but not without a weapon to protect myself," Tyson remarked.

Tyson's willingness to volunteer startled his uncle. "You can't go out there," Dino firmly insisted. "You know what happened to the others. It's not safe."

"I know it's not the smartest thing," Tyson informed him, "but if there are injured people on that bus, maybe we can bring them back to the hotel and treat their injuries. You can't just leave them out there like that."

"Well, if he's going then so am I," Sonya bluntly announced while folding her arms across her chest.

"This is insane. You're all going to get killed," Dino bellowed then looked at Ravin and pointed at him. "You're supposed to be the smart one. Tell them!"

Ravin looked from Dino to the others and took a deep, reluctant breath. "I would, but I'm going with them."

Dino shook his head while attempting to hold back his nervous laugh. "You're all insane. You're going to end up just like the others."

"Unlike you, Mayor Dino," Vander announced, "we're not afraid of ghosts."

"Maybe you should be," Dino launched back. "You may want to think about that."

Vander nodded the others toward the main door across the lobby. Tyson grabbed a decorative brass candlestick from the hall table as a crude weapon and hurried after the others. Dino watched them leave and again shook his head.

"Stupid know-it-alls," he muttered.

Chapter Sixteen

The eight men and women walked along the path in the woods with Vander and Novak leading the way. They exchanged words more quietly now, but neither was about to let what happened that morning go. Sonya clung to Ravin and was moderately flirtatious, although Ravin was obviously disinterested. Whatever fueled his hormones only seemed to apply to Gemma. Devon walked alongside Tyson and kept close watch on the woods surrounding them. She could see the spirits just ahead still roaming around aimlessly. Tyson was a talker and readily shared his life with her. He was easy to read, in her opinion, which seemed odd in itself. Considering their current situation at the hotel, he didn't feel nearly as cluttered as the others did. The vibes she got from him were no different from any other guy she'd ever met. She could sense he was moderately attracted to her, although he didn't exactly hide that fact. Compared to the others, he seemed almost normal. Whatever was happening around the hotel didn't seem to affect him as severely as the others. She wondered what factored that.

"This used to be a wonderful place to live," Tyson told Devon, snapping her out of her trance. He grinned boyishly. "I had a great childhood here."

"Used to be wonderful? What happened?" she asked.

"The hotel happened," he replied dryly with a soft sigh. "Tourists flooded the town during the best seasons and drove away most of the locals."

"So almost all the dead people worked at the hotel?" Devon questioned.

"Just about," he informed her. He glanced over her, admired her figure, and then smiled charmingly. "You, uh, with any of these bozos?"

"I'm only with them--not with them," she replied almost teasingly.

Devon realized what she said and hoped he didn't take that as an invitation. Although undeniably handsome, he wasn't her type. For her, that wasn't just a calculated guess. His sexual vibe was very strong. He'd been around the block several times and with many women. She could sense that settling down with just one woman wasn't in his immediate future.

Tyson eyed her, appeared pleased, and chuckled softly. "Happy to hear," he teased. "Believe me; I'm not nearly as crazy as the others."

"So you've noticed changes in their personalities?" Devon asked with surprise.

"Absolutely," he replied. "When that basket case Gemma isn't flipping out, she and Ravin are going at it like bunnies on ecstasy. My balls of brass uncle claims he's been talking to my dead mother, who, by the way, still wonders why she has no grandkids, and my sister insists there are monsters under her bed." He shook his head with disgust. "Then there's the 'sexually impaired' Felicia coming on to every man like Lassie in heat. I swear everyone around me is either paranoid, aggressive, or hornier than hell. And when you put them together in a combo pack--look out. I feel like the designated driver at Woodstock."

"That's probably more accurate than you think," she replied with a defeated sigh. She eyed him suspiciously. "But you haven't shown any symptoms like the others?"

He snorted a laugh, humored by the comment. "Well, living out here in the middle of butt-nut nowhere, hornier than hell is pretty common for any normal, healthy man. Women don't grow on trees in the sticks, but I can't say I've noticed any changes in my mood." His smile mocked her. "Although, I suppose when someone goes crazy, they're the last to know, huh?" He grinned at his own joke. "Unlike the others, I haven't seen any ghosts."

"So why were you agreeing with the others last night?" she asked.

"If my uncle says he sees ghosts, you agree there are ghosts," Tyson replied. "It's not worth suffering his wrath to disagree with him. He'll just lecture endlessly until you cave. In his mind, he's never wrong. You've met him. Would you want to get into a debate with him over, well, anything?"

Devon laughed softly. "No, I suppose not. I have an aunt like that. We should get them together."

Tyson came across as a nice country boy with a natural respect toward women. Despite his experience with many women, he was certainly a step above Harris and his perverted tendencies. Sonya, on the other hand, was displaying the extremes Tyson had mentioned. His sister was crawling all over Ravin, who didn't react either way to her probing hands. Devon could feel Sonya's emotions, and they were all over the place. She and Gemma apparently had a lot in common at the moment. There was an odd twitchiness about Sonya. She was a ticking time bomb, and poor Ravin had to contend with her. Then there was Darlene. Moderately paranoid, the young woman was managing to keep a level head on their hike through what Dino considered hostile territory. Dino was in a class by himself, in Devon's opinion. He was levelheaded, commanding, and displayed above average intelligence, but his paranoia surpassed everyone else's. He just hid it better.

Vander and Novak stopped suddenly, alerting the others. Everyone stopped and stared at the sight before them. More than ten men hung by their necks from trees in the woods. They were cut open from groin to sternum with their innards lying in a sloppy pile on the ground below them. They resembled drown rats from being exposed to the torrential downpours, leaving their hollowed out centers grotesquely clean. Sonya screamed hysterically at the sight and clung to Ravin. Ravin was barely fazed as he stared at the dead men with little expression.

"That's how we found them yesterday morning," Ravin informed the others. He indicated the more severely decomposed man. It was Anderson. "That's one of the men the town sent out before the others came to the hotel to stay." He nodded to the others. "Those were the ones who went for help over the last two days."

Reed's body was seen hanging from a tree as well. It was a sobering image for everyone. As Devon stared at Reed, she saw images flashing through her mind of him being hoisted up the tree with the noose around his neck. He didn't struggle but his flinching suggested he was still alive while being hanged. There was a flash of a hunting knife piercing his sternum and being dragged down to his groin. He didn't flinch, but she knew he felt the pain of the knife penetrating deep into his body and the slicing as it cut him open. There was blood and internal organs spilling out and onto the ground with the most hideous plopping sound. Death followed shortly thereafter. Other images similar to Reed's flooded her senses. They were all alive while being hanged and gutted. They all felt the torturous pain. Devon could almost feel the knife slicing into her midsection. She suddenly gasped and clutched her pounding head. She had to stop the images! It was too much! For a moment, she only heard the sound of her own heart pounding. Tyson became concerned, placed his arms around her, and helped steady her. She anxiously looked up at Reed where he hung from the tree, completely hollowed out. His ghost stared back at her with the same confused look as the others.

Devon looked at the other spirits lingering around the area. They were all staring at her as well. She muttered softly, "Now I understand--"

Tyson stared at Devon while he held her. "Huh?"

She shook her head and attempted to pull away from him. "Nothing."

The images subsided, and she was free from the agonizing pain. Tyson reluctantly released her. There was movement within the woods, alerting everyone. Vander and Novak removed their guns and aimed them toward the source of the sound. A German shepherd dog appeared on the path before them. Everyone groaned softly at the panting, happy dog. Vander and Novak replaced their guns while attempting to relax.

"We should get moving," Vander said.

"You still want to continue?" Ravin asked with a surprised look on his face.

"Make no mistake, I want to run into the bastard who did this," Vander informed him.

The dog took off into the woods. Everyone looked up as they passed the hanging bodies. They could clearly identify each man's face. Apart from their hollowed out insides, there was no indication of how they had died. Only Devon knew the gruesome details of their last moments. Had they been lucky, being hanged would have been what killed them, but sadly, that wasn't the case. Being gutted killed them. Again, why they didn't defend themselves was the mystery. Trent suddenly appeared on the path before them, startling everyone. He was surprised to see the four familiar faces then looked relieved.

"Thank God I found you," Trent gasped while out of breath. Harris and Trent exchanged a manly hug, happy to see each other. "I got turned around in the woods following that damned dog." Trent noticed the bodies hanging from the trees and suddenly jumped backwards, nearly falling down. "Oh, shit!"

"Don't ask," Harris muttered.

Trent couldn't tear his eyes away from the image but refrained from comment at Harris' suggestion.

"Was Monica able to treat the injured people on the bus?" Vander asked him.

He looked at Vander with the horror evident in his eyes. "You won't believe it," Trent said softly. "They're all dead."

The others were stunned.

"Dead? How?" Harris demanded, having been hit particularly hard by the news. Most of the men on the party bus were their longtime friends.

"Someone or something killed them," Trent quickly said. "Monica and I were on our way to the hotel last night when this dog appeared and scared the shit out of us. Since we didn't know if "Jack the Ripper" was still out there, we decided to stay in that abandoned town last night. Monica went back to the bus this morning, insisting she needed to find some answers, but she never returned." He looked at the hanging bodies and shook his head while attempting to keep from trembling. "Something is seriously messed up around here."

"You haven't heard the worst of it," Novak remarked.

Trent suddenly looked at him and was stunned. "What's worse than a bus full of mutilated people and a forest with gutted men hanging from trees?"

"A hotel full of dead people," Darlene muttered.

"If the people from the crash are all dead, we should go back to the hotel," Sonya pleaded.

"I'm with the young lady," Trent announced. "The road is completely flooded behind the wreck. Even if we hiked out to the flooded main road, it's twenty miles or more before we'd reach any kind of help."

"There's no help at the hotel. That place is a death trap," Vander informed him. "The rest of you can go back, but Novak and I are hiking to the nearest town."

Novak suddenly looked at Vander with wide, horror-filled eyes. "Yeah, I'm really not okay with that, Vander."

Vander glared his disapproval at Novak.

Darlene looked down the path then glanced at the others. "If I can get to the farm on the other side of town, my friend's horse is in the pasture," she informed them. "I can ride through the shallow end of the ravine and across the flooded areas. I can cover the twenty miles a lot faster than if you hiked."

"That's an excellent plan, but I should go," Vander informed her.

"Do you ride much, Agent Hawk?" Darlene asked him with a curious look.

"When I was young."

"I can ride, and I can ride fast," Darlene said.

"Fine," Vander groaned softly. "I'll give you an escort as far as the ravine."

"You can give me an escort to the farm," she announced firmly. "Once I'm on the horse, you'll only slow me down."

Vander stared at Darlene a moment, reluctantly frowned, and then turned to Novak. "Take everyone back to the hotel. I'll go with Darlene to the farm and see her off."

"You shouldn't go alone, Agent Hawk," Devon suddenly announced then glanced at the spirits staring back at her near where the dead men hanged.

Devon wanted to tell him what she knew, but she couldn't. He'd never believe her. She wished she knew why it was so important that she protect him. He must later play an important role in catching the killer or even protecting her. She kept her mind closed. She couldn't allow any more images into her head. She already felt as if her head was about to split open. Vander stared at Devon a moment and attempted to read her. She knew how she must have come across. She knew her look was that of a crazy woman. It couldn't be helped. She almost had herself convinced she actually was crazy. If he wouldn't listen to her, she'd have to confess everything to keep him from traveling alone. For some reason, it was that important.

"I'll go with him," Tyson boldly announced with little hesitation. "I know these woods better than anyone here. I think I prefer being outside and away from that hotel for a while anyway."

"Fine," Vander remarked. "Tyson's with us. The rest of you follow Ravin back to the hotel."

Tyson smacked Vander on the shoulder and grinned. "Let's go, G-man."

Devon shut her eyes and felt oddly relieved. Safety in numbers was no guarantee, but it was safer than Vander going alone. As

Tyson, Vander, and Darlene headed for town, Devon felt compelled to look back while following her own group. Something strange stirred within her. An image attempted to enter her head, but she refused to let it in. Vander looked back, caught her stare, and offered a tiny smile. She felt compelled to smile back and subsequently blushed having been caught looking back. As she followed the others, something suddenly occurred to her. Perhaps her concern for him had nothing to do with ghosts, safety, or even catching a killer. Maybe she just thought he was cute.

Chapter Seventeen

$\mathcal{V}$ander and Tyson stood near the old, large barn and watched Darlene ride the stocky, black horse at a canter across the field toward the distant ravine. She wasn't bragging; she knew how to ride and was quickly able to cover the grassy terrain. Once she made it past the ravine and the flooded roadway, she'd have a straight shot for the nearest inhabited town. A rescue was at most several hours away. Tyson grinned lustfully and shook his head while snatching his bottle of water from the ground near the hitching post.

"I don't know about you, but there's just something about a woman's ass slapping a leather saddle that gets me all hot," Tyson announced.

Vander glared at Tyson.

Tyson eyed the disapproving look he received from Vander and chuckled. "Loosen up, G-man. We're not long for this world. May as well go out with a bang," he announced then took a swallow from his bottle of water and lustfully raised his brows. "And I know what I'd like to be banging right about now."

"Are we seriously having this conversation?" Vander demanded. "I can't believe you're preoccupied with sexual fantasies after that massacre at the hotel."

Tyson shrugged. "It'd be nice getting laid once more before someone whacks me. Nothing wrong with a man wanting that, is there?" He slapped Vander's shoulder then gave it an oddly firm squeeze. "Come on, I'm sure even uptight feds like you get the urge now and again."

Vander rolled his eyes, refusing to partake in the conversation, and then noticed the bottle of water Tyson held. He looked around the area surrounding the hitching post then glared at Tyson. "Is that my water you're drinking?"

"Nope, I got this from your pretty lady friend," he announced cheerfully and grinned. "I think she likes me."

"I doubt you're her type, but good luck with that," Vander muttered.

Vander looked around the area surrounding the barn, recovered his own bottle of water, and headed across the pasture in the direction of town. Tyson retrieved his candlestick. He casually followed after Vander with a lively spring in his step after having entertained a sexual fantasy or two undoubtedly involving Devon. Vander didn't seem to want anything to do with the country boy on the return trip and attempted to ignore him. Tyson was tough to ignore.

"So, uh, about that girl with you--" he announced.

"No," Vander replied without waiting for the question, "I don't know if she's seeing anyone."

"Actually, I was going to ask if she was into anything, you know, kinky, but I'm guessing you have no idea. She looks a little devilish, don't you think?"

Vander appeared stunned and looked at Tyson with his mouth hanging open. "What's wrong with you?"

"Just hoping to get lucky," Tyson casually replied. "Aren't we all?"

"I'm just hoping to survive long enough to forget this conversation," Vander muttered.

"Oh, I see," he announced cheerfully. "You have a hard on for the little temptress."

"We're not discussing this," Vander firmly announced.

Tyson chuckled softly and took another swig of water. Vander eyed him suspiciously. Apparently, that boy-next-door act was just a well-rehearsed show to get into Devon's pants.

"It's okay, G-man," Tyson announced, "I know you have an image to uphold. She won't hear about your hard on from me."

†

*T*he hotel seemed peaceful in the early morning hours. The sun was shining, and it was going to be a beautiful day. Unfortunately, none within the hotel would be in the mood to enjoy the sunny afternoon approaching. Gunshots suddenly echoed from the woods and broke the silence. Novak, Devon, Ravin, and Sonya stepped through the main doors and looked around the resort grounds with concern. Nothing moved and the surrounding acreage was eerily silent. Vander and Tyson suddenly appeared from the woods and ran across the clearing toward the hotel in a state of panic. Vander had his gun clutched in his hand, obviously having been the one firing the shots. Both men stopped near the hotel and the others while breathing heavily.

Tyson suddenly looked at Vander. Anger swept over him as he straightened and attempted to control his panting. "What the hell were you shooting at?" he demanded.

"Didn't you see it?" Vander exclaimed.

"See what?" Tyson cried out. "I was too busy ducking for cover and running!"

Vander replaced his gun to his shoulder holster and looked disgusted.

"Son-of-a-bitch!" Tyson exploded while rubbing his chest as he breathed heavily. "Give a guy a little warning before you go shooting off your gun like that!"

"Maybe if you'd shut your mouth for more than thirty seconds--" Vander scoffed.

Novak stood alongside Devon and looked at both men with surprise. "What's going on?" he suddenly demanded of his partner. "What were you shooting at?"

"I saw something in the trees by the hanging bodies," Vander informed him. "Whatever it was, it looked like it was eating the flesh from the corpses."

Tyson suddenly straightened and glared at Vander. "You idiot!" he snapped. "It was probably some wild animal. The woods are full of them!"

He suddenly glared at Tyson with limited patience. "You're calling me an idiot?" Vander demanded.

"That's enough, Tyson," Sonya announced sternly. "Don't make me call Uncle Dino."

"Fine," Tyson snapped then glared at Vander.

Sonya pulled him past the others toward the hotel.

Tyson saw Devon as they passed, gave her a quick once over, and grinned lustfully. "Have any plans for this evening, sexy?" he asked.

Without warning, Novak punched Tyson in the mouth, sending him stumbling backwards and away from Sonya's grip. Despite his surprise, Tyson quickly recovered and lunged for Novak. They punched each other without provocation. Ravin placed his hands in his pockets and calmly watched the two men fight only a few feet in front of him. Dino appeared from the hotel, saw the men fighting, and ran toward them. Dino and Vander pulled the two men apart. Dino had his arm firmly around Tyson's neck and pulled him toward the hotel while softly scolding him.

Vander held Novak back and stared at him with surprise. "What the hell was that?"

"He came on to my girlfriend," Novak snapped. "You saw him!"

Devon stared at Novak with surprise and possible alarm. Had she heard him correctly? She wasn't sure what was happening, but it would seem Novak had been adversely affected. How was it even possible?

"Your what?" Vander suddenly demanded, sharing Devon's confusion.

"That prick came on to my girlfriend!"

Vander shook his head with disbelief while staring at Novak. "What the hell are you talking about? She's *not* your girlfriend," he informed him sternly.

"You're jealous, admit it," Novak snorted with annoyance and turned aggressive for no apparent reason. "You want her for yourself, don't you?"

Without warning, Novak punched Vander in the face. Vander was momentarily stunned then glared at his friend. Novak immediately took another swing. Vander blocked his punch and struck him. Both men punched each other without cause. Devon looked at Ravin, who casually watched with little reaction as he stood alongside her. It didn't appear if anyone else intended to step in and break it up. Devon stepped into the fight, grabbed Vander's arm, and stopped him from swinging. She knew she was taking a huge risk by getting between the two highly trained fighters. Novak held back his punch when he saw Devon in his path.

Vander immediately relaxed, pulled Devon to his side, and glared at Novak. "Stay the hell away from her," Vander scoffed and pointed a warning finger at his partner. "She's my girlfriend and don't you forget it."

Devon looked at Vander with a shocked expression. Novak became enraged and lunged for Vander. Novak was suddenly tackled to the ground by a dark blur, startling everyone. Monica gracefully rolled off Novak and onto her feet.

"What the hell is wrong with you two?" Monica suddenly demanded while looking at both men. She'd obviously been across the grounds when the fight broke out and saw the entire thing going down.

Novak sprang to his feet, glared at Monica with hostility, and pointed a warning finger at her then shouted, "This doesn't concern you, bitch!"

"Bitch?" Monica growled with a look on her face that immediately frightened Devon.

Without warning, Monica punched Novak in the face. Novak stumbled back a step while holding his face. He glared at Monica with surprise.

"Call me bitch again, and you'll be spitting out teeth," Monica snarled at him.

Novak sneered and punched Monica in the face. Devon cried out with horror while placing her hand to her mouth. She couldn't believe Novak, a federal agent, punched a woman! Monica slowly turned her head and looked at Novak with a slightly psychotic look that alarmed everyone.

"Okay, now you pissed me off," Monica snarled lowly.

Monica spun into a roundhouse kick and knocked Novak back several steps. He regained his balance and karate kicked back at her. The two punched and kicked each other with great skill and precision. Devon and Vander watched with some surprise. Ravin maintained his same, emotionless expression and was unaffected either way. As they watched the two kick and punch each other, Vander took Devon's hand in his. She was oblivious to him holding her hand and concentrated on the ensuing fight. She couldn't believe no one was willing to break it up, and she knew she wasn't getting between the two. More importantly, she couldn't believe Monica was holding her own! Vander casually placed Devon's hand to his crotch. Devon suddenly looked at him with surprise and pulled her hand away. Novak finally collapsed to the ground in near exhaustion and slowly moved to his knees. He looked up at Monica while breathing heavily. Monica glared down at him and raised a cocky brow as if waiting for either an apology or an announcement of submission. Despite Novak's exhaustion, Monica wasn't nearly as winded.

Novak stared up at her and grinned. "You are *so* hot."

Monica sneered and punched him across the face. Novak hit the ground and was down for the count.

Chapter Eighteen

$\mathcal{R}$avin calmly stood over Novak, who sat in an oversized lobby chair while holding an ice pack to his mouth. Monica had nailed him good, and the large bruise on his face supported her fighting skills were superior to his. Vander paced near them and watched Devon while she talked to Monica at the other end of the lobby. He resembled a predator stalking its prey, never once taking his eyes off Devon. Novak lowered his ice pack and watched the women as well, seemingly sharing Vander's expression. They were both suddenly mutts in heat, and it wasn't going to end well for either if they acted upon that instinct.

"I don't know what they're saying, but it's really turning me on," Novak muttered softly.

Ravin followed Novak's stare to Monica across the room. He seemed mildly disinterested and looked back at him. "You may want to keep those thoughts to yourself," he remarked casually then indicated Monica with a slight nod. "That one will undoubtedly kill you."

"Hmm, feisty and sexy," Novak said while groaning lustfully without taking his eyes off her.

Just across the lobby, Monica stared at Devon with a look of surprise on her face as her mouth hung open. "Are they *all* hallucinating?"

"Hallucinating and wild mood swings too," Devon informed her. "Novak freaked out early this morning, but Vander didn't start acting strange until they returned from their little expedition." Devon remained tense and glanced at the three men across the lobby. The way they stared back chilled her. She looked back at Monica while insecurely rubbing her arms. "Since you and Trent weren't affected, it has to be something in the hotel," she insisted. "Something they've ingested recently."

"I don't understand," Monica announced. "If it's something they've ingested within the hotel, why haven't you been affected? Haven't you been drinking the same stuff?"

Devon frowned and carefully considered how to respond to the question. She came up with an acceptable version of the truth that didn't make her sound completely insane. "Drugs and alcohol don't really affect me. I've always been that way," she replied. "It's *difficult* to explain."

"That must blow," Monica muttered. She glanced across the lobby to the three men who watched them intensely. "Jesus, why do I feel like they're sizing us up for dinner?"

"Lust seems to be a major symptom among all of them," Devon remarked lowly. "And I know what you're thinking, but it's not just the men. Gemma, Sonya, and Felicia are all showing signs of sexual aggression." She then considered the comment. "Darlene didn't seem to be affected."

"Great, it's boot camp all over again," Monica retorted then assessed the situation while studying the three men. She finally looked back at Devon. "If one of them will let me examine and question them, I might be able to tell what drug we're dealing with and isolate it."

"I'm going to recommend you keep a safe distance from Agent Delano right now," Devon informed her in a serious tone. "He obviously has eyes for you, and I wouldn't doubt his hands will soon follow."

"Yeah? Well, I have fists for him," Monica muttered and cracked her knuckles.

"Exactly why you should avoid him," she replied then gently cleared her throat. "I'd prefer it if you didn't kill a federal agent while we're stuck here." Devon studied Ravin from across the lobby.

"Ravin's been completely rational and hasn't shown any signs of aggression. He's definitely been affected, but he's kept it under control. Well, except when he gets together with Gemma. Then it's wild kingdom. I don't even want to imagine what those two do behind closed doors."

Monica seemed surprised and raised her brows in question. "That meek guy?"

"Oh, yeah," Devon replied. "I heard he's a stud muffin. Of course, that is coming from a woman seemingly flying high on ecstasy."

"It's always the quiet ones," Monica remarked and shook her head. "He's probably into whips and chains."

"Hmm, somehow I don't think so," Devon casually replied. "I think he's your safest bet."

"I'll trust your judgment. We should see if the hotel has an infirmary or nurse's office," Monica informed her. "It'll have everything I need to examine him. Maybe I can figure out what we're dealing with."

†

*R*avin sat in the chair before the desk in the infirmary. He had a digital thermometer in his mouth. Monica scanned his eyes for pupillary responses with a penlight she'd found. She removed the thermometer and asked him a series of questions relating to how he felt. She then proceeded to take his blood pressure. Vander stood casually in the doorway and keep close watch over Devon, who assisted Monica. Devon knew he was watching her, making her uncomfortable, but she refused to look at him to avoid any further issues. Monica's line of questioning must have peaked Vander's curiosity, focusing his attention on her instead.

"If it's something in the hotel, why haven't the rest of us been affected?" Vander asked simply.

Devon and Monica exchanged looks. He really had no clue to his own behavior. Devon couldn't believe how quickly Vander had transformed. Although he seemed fine at the moment, she was convinced it wouldn't take much to wind him up. Monica finished her exam of her exceptionally cooperative patient.

"Will I live?" Ravin teased.

"If you don't piss off your girlfriend again, I think you'll survive," Monica replied and indicated the healing scratches he'd received.

Ravin insecurely touched the scratches on his neck and cringed slightly. "She thought I'd turned into a zombie. I'm sure it was my fault," he insisted. "I should probably work on my tan this summer."

Monica stared at him with surprise and raised her brows. "You're a keeper," she replied then looked at Devon. "I can't be positive, but my guess is LSD." Monica then grinned at Ravin. "Enjoy your trip."

He appeared surprised while staring at her. "That causes hallucinations," Ravin announced then sank into thought. "That certainly would explain most of what's happening around here, but how was it introduced? After the others were poisoned, we were very careful about what we ate and drank. We even stopped drinking the tap water."

"You could be tripping up to ten hours on a single dose," Monica informed him, "but with your symptoms; I'm guessing you've been exposed to the drug recently and often."

"Recently and often?" Ravin gasped with surprise. "The only thing I've had in the last twenty-four hours is bottled water, canned fruit, and wine. There are hundreds of bottles in the wine cellar. It sounds improbable."

"So it's probably not the wine," Monica replied. "Someone could have soaked the tops of unopened water bottles in the drug. Enough of it would seep through to the mouthpiece to cause mild exposure." She casually stood then sank into thought. "Continued use would easily cause what we're seeing here."

"We've all been drinking the bottled water," Ravin informed her with skepticism. "I don't see how that would benefit the perpetrator."

"I'm sure whoever is responsible has their own, untainted supply," Vander informed him and straightened. "I drank the water, and I'm fine."

Devon and Monica eyed Vander with surprise and again exchanged looks. Monica shook her head and attempted to hide her mocking grin.

"We should boil the water bottles," Monica suggested. "It'll sterilize them and dissolve the drugs."

"There are some in the refrigerator and several cases in the pantry," Ravin informed her.

"We can drink wine in the meantime," Monica announced. "Obviously, if the bottles are dusty, we know they haven't been tampered with."

"So in ten hours, everyone should be back to normal?" Devon asked.

"More or less," Monica replied. "Why don't you go with Ravin and get some wine. Agent Hawk and I will start boiling the water bottles."

Vander glanced lustfully over Devon then looked at Monica. "Or you could go with Ravin to the wine cellar, and I'll go with Devon."

Monica glared her disapproval at Vander and folded her arms across her chest. "Or I could kick you in the nuts, and we can call it a day."

Vander frowned.

Chapter Nineteen

*R*avin stood before one of the racks within the wine cellar and handed Devon dusty bottles of wine. She placed them into a crate on the floor by her feet. The crate was nearly filled with a dozen bottles of wine. He suddenly stopped and stared blankly at the bottle in his hand. Devon glanced at him and wondered what world he was slipping into now. She could tell he was conflicted, but she wasn't getting a clear vibe from him.

"I'm going to lose her, aren't I?" Ravin said softly.

"Excuse me?"

"Gemma," he faintly replied. "I'm going to lose her once the drugs wear off." He frowned and shook his head. "Somewhere deep down, I knew she was never really mine."

"You don't know what will happen, Ravin," Devon said gently. "Monica thinks the drugs enhance whatever emotions you're already feeling. There's no guarantee you'll lose her."

"It's not just the mind-blowing sex I'll miss, you know," he announced with conviction. "I feel as if we've been together forever." Ravin glanced at her and seemed curious. "Will I remember feeling that? Or will it all go away too?"

"I wish I could answer that," Devon replied. She felt bad for Ravin. He already seemed burdened with losing the young woman he hadn't even lost yet. "The drugs seem to overstimulate sexual responses. The men seem to be hit particularly hard by the drug's effects."

"Well, that would explain your three new boyfriends," he announced and managed a soft laugh. He seemed particularly amused. "It's pretty sad that men can be reduced to steaming piles of testosterone." Ravin handed Devon the bottle and pulled out another. There was a strange silence. "Are you sure it's drugs?" Ravin looked at her and appeared curious. "I mean, you're obviously an attractive woman, but I don't feel the need to hump you like a mutt in heat. If it was drugs, shouldn't I be all over you as well? That has to mean something, don't you think?"

"Maybe," she replied and gave him a curious look. "Were you attracted to Gemma before?"

"Of course," Ravin replied without hesitation then smiled dreamily. "Did I ever tell you about my first date with Gemma? It was late last summer. We had a romantic, sunset picnic on the beach--"

Devon muttered, "And another lucid moment passes."

$$\dagger$$

*D*evon and Ravin walked along the grand hallway after their side trip to the kitchen to deposit the case of wine. Ravin had been particularly quiet after a longwinded story of graphic sex with Gemma on their non-existent picnic last summer. Even without any psychic abilities, those images were going to be stuck in her mind a long time. On the bright side, it sounded like Gemma was in capable hands. Ravin portrayed himself to be quite the proficient lover. As they walked along the hall, they saw the dining room door standing open, catching their attention. They exchanged bewildered looks.

"Wasn't that locked?" Devon asked.

"Yes," he replied with added concern. "I locked it myself after your friends did their investigation."

They cautiously approached the open doors and looked inside. Ravin and Devon slowly entered the dining room. The dead, decaying bodies were repositioned neatly in the chairs before the tables. They looked almost natural, sending concern through both. Devon was especially chilled by the freaky scene. When one of the corpses moved, Devon jumped with a horrified gasp. Ravin was immediately alerted to her observation. Upon closer inspection, she realized it was Felicia and not one of the corpses. Felicia sat at one of the tables while conversing with a dead, decaying woman slumped over the table.

"I was so worried about you," Felicia said with sincerity to the dead woman. "I thought you were actually dead. Thank God that wasn't the case." She giggled in a chilling manner. "I'm feeling pretty stupid about that now."

Devon glanced at the ghost of the dead woman, who just stared at Felicia with a bewildered look. Even the dead woman's ghost thought Felicia was acting strange. The feeling Devon was getting from Felicia conveyed her confused state of mind. She was in denial that those within the dining room were dead, and she had no fear of her current situation. Devon was so engrossed with what she was witnessing; she hadn't even noticed a few of the ghosts moving closer to her. She finally became aware of what was happening as the remaining ghosts collected around her. It was a new first for her and not in a good way. She insecurely rubbed her chilled arms while staring at the ghosts surrounding her. They stared at her with puzzled looks and seemed to be waiting for her to answer their silent questions. She wasn't sure what she could say to them, although she wasn't about to speak to them in front of Ravin. She needed to keep him as grounded as possible right now.

"I'm a little disturbed by this," Ravin said softly.

"Yes, it's disturbing on many levels," Devon replied while looking at the ghosts surrounding her. She shifted her attention away from the ghosts and onto Felicia seated at the table with the dead woman. "Felicia?" Devon gently said. She didn't acknowledge Devon. "Felicia--"

Felicia suddenly glared at Devon with irritation and possible hostility. "Can't you see I'm talking to my friend," she snarled. "Go away!"

Devon was surprised by the sudden outburst. Whatever drugs were coursing through Felicia's veins had taken her to a whole other level. There would be no reasoning with her as long as she was in her current frame of mind.

Ravin gently took Devon by the arm. "We should probably do as she says," he announced softly. "She can be a little unstable at times."

"I'm not about to argue that," Devon replied.

She knew his comment to be true just by what she was feeling from Felicia. At the moment, she was contented just to talk to her dead friend, but her aggressiveness was lurking just beyond the surface. It wouldn't take much for her to react violently. Ravin guided her from the dining room.

"I caught her and Cody going at it in the kitchen last evening before you and your friends arrived," he informed Devon. "She'd been climbing all over him that entire afternoon. Quite the spectacle, I'll tell you."

Devon eyed him with surprise. He didn't even seem aware of his own public sexual exploits with Gemma.

"I attempted to sneak away unnoticed when I heard a crash," he announced. "When I looked back, she was beating the hell out of him. There they were, both naked, her chasing him around the kitchen like a woman scorned." He shook his head. "Like nothing I'd ever seen before."

"Maybe she thought he turned into a zombie," Devon teased and immediately scolded herself for making light of the incident.

Ravin stopped her in the dining room doorway, turned to face her, and stared with a serious look on his face. "You know, the exact same thing happened with Gemma."

Devon smiled gently and pulled Ravin from the dining room.

Chapter Twenty

$\mathcal{V}$ander, Ravin, Monica, and Devon followed the overly anxious Harris onto the third floor balcony where Dino and Cody stood while casually leaning against the railing. Despite the beautiful, warm day, the two men didn't appear pleased with what they had seen.

"You're not going to like this," Harris announced as he herded the others toward the balcony railing.

All five approached the brothers and scanned the surrounding resort grounds in an attempt to see what had everyone looking bothered. Dino handed Vander a pair of binoculars with the disgust evident on his face and pointed across the countryside toward the remains of the old church.

"Out by the old church," Dino said.

Vander looked through the binoculars. The saddled, black horse grazed among the cemetery headstones just beyond what was left of the church ruins. There was blood on the saddle, indicating something unforeseen had happened to its rider. Darlene was nowhere to be found. There was no telling how long the horse had been roaming free, but it was obvious Darlene had met her fate somewhere on the other side of town. Undoubtedly, she was ambushed not long after Vander and Tyson had left her. Vander frowned and furiously returned the binoculars to Dino. Cody was quick to accept them on his behalf.

"Son-of-a-bitch!" Vander proclaimed and slammed his hand on the railing. "I knew I shouldn't have let her go! I knew it was a bad idea, but I let her talk me into it!"

Dino's mood matched Vander's mood as he glared at him. "I told you not to leave the hotel," Dino growled lowly. "You knew others who had tried never made it. Maybe if you'd listened to me in the first place, Darlene wouldn't be dead."

Vander glared at Dino and showed his hostility to the comment. "Your big plan is to sit around and let some psycho killer pick us off one by one. How's that working out for you?"

Dino turned to face Vander with an unpredictable look of hostility in his eyes. Vander immediately straightened defensively. The standoff was chilling.

"I *cared* about that woman," Dino launched back.

"Then maybe you should have stopped her," Vander snapped.

Devon felt her entire body twitch. Someone had to stop their argument from turning into a fistfight, because the outcome would be disastrous. She could just imagine someone flying over the railing to their death on the patio several stories below.

"You want to do this, Agent Hawk?" Dino suddenly lashed out. "We'll do this!"

Monica suddenly stepped between them and held a hand to both their chests. Devon felt the horror sweep through her. She wasn't sure if Monica was good enough to take on Dino, who was roughly the size of a tank.

"If you boys want to settle something, I'll be more than happy to settle it for you," Monica announced with a hostile look in her eyes. "Now stand down."

Dino snorted a laugh and looked at Monica with obvious humor. He could undoubtedly crush her like a toothpick. "Give it your best shot--"

Monica suddenly grabbed Dino's crotch, dropping him to his knees in a split second. She released him as he fell and stared down at him while he clutched himself in agony. "You don't want to see my best shot," she informed him gruffly then turned to Vander and raised her brows. "How about you?"

Vander quickly took a step back while holding his hands over his crotch. "No, I'm good."

107

Monica snatched the binoculars from Cody, stood before the railing, and stared out at the distant cemetery. She seemed oblivious to Dino's glare as he straightened behind her. There was a good chance he wasn't about to let that confrontation pass without repercussions. Cody immediately placed his hands on his brother's shoulders from behind and reined him in. Devon was finally able to breathe again. Ravin's lack of emotion to any of what happened was concerning to Devon. She didn't sense anything from him. Was he intentionally blocking her from reading him, or did he really have no emotions to share? She'd wasted enough time trying to figure out the odd, little man and returned her attention to what was important at the moment. Their dire situation.

"What now?" Devon asked.

Vander sank into thought while staring across the resort grounds at the distant remains of the old church. He appeared disgusted and shook his head. "I have to go out there, get that horse, and try to make it to the nearest town," Vander informed them.

The thought horrified Devon. It didn't work for Darlene, and she was nearly two miles from the hotel when she almost certainly met her fate. That close to the hotel, Vander would be an easy target for a sniper hiding in the woods.

"No one has made it out of here," Cody announced sternly. "We need to wait it out until help comes. The flooded roadways will be passible soon. A day or two at most. No one else needs to risk their lives."

"He's right, Agent Hawk," Devon said gently while fighting that odd feeling she couldn't seem to shake. "You're more valuable to us alive here than dead out there."

Vander glanced at Devon and stared longer than he should have, making her uncomfortable. He seemed in control of his emotions and didn't send any sexual vibes as he had earlier. Perhaps whatever drugs were coursing through his system had already worn off.

Vander considered her comment then reluctantly groaned. "Fine, one more day," he remarked sternly, giving in to the mounting pressure that no one else should leave.

Ravin glanced at his watch and was surprised by the time. "Oh, it's one o'clock."

Vander glared at him and seemed instantly annoyed. "Have a hot date?" he demanded.

He looked innocently at Vander. "Gemma and I are taking a bubble bath at one," Ravin announced then grinned at Vander and Devon while lustfully raising his brows in suggestion. "You two should try it. Very stimulating."

Vander glanced at Devon. She caught his look and feared what he was thinking or what thoughts the suggestion might bring. Vander hid his smile and looked away. Devon felt relief throughout her entire body. Agent Hawk was back to his old, strait-laced self. She was glade there wouldn't be any more awkward encounters like there had been earlier.

✝

*D*evon sat at the island counter alongside Vander, who'd remained an absolute saint the last two hours. Despite his return to Mr. FBI, Devon still couldn't relax around him. She remained tense while drinking a glass of wine. She wished the wine affected her the same as it did most people, but there was no sedating effect for her. It was just fermented grapes. She desperately wanted to feel relaxed. Perhaps she did need a hot bubble bath. She assumed that was the stimulation most people felt when they drank. Since alcohol didn't affect her, she'd never know. Monica searched the cupboards while wearing a pair of surgical gloves from the infirmary. She'd been busily searching the cupboards for nearly thirty minutes now. The woman was on a mission and enjoyed keeping busy. Devon was convinced Monica would make an excellent detective. Monica removed an old metal can, smelled inside it, and made a face.

"I found your poison," Monica announced.

Vander looked up with surprise. "Really? Excellent. Bag that for me," he replied.

Monica placed it in a large, zip lock bag and set it aside. She continued to rummage through the cupboards and removed a strange looking canister. She studied it with a bewildered look.

"What the hell--?"

Monica returned to the cupboard and dug deeper into the back. Vander refilled Devon's wineglass, grinned lustfully, and gently caressed her leg. Devon jumped with surprise. Perhaps he wasn't back to his old self after all. She removed his hand from her leg. If his plan was to get her drunk, he was in for a surprise. Novak entered the kitchen and eyed Monica's posterior view as she stretched for the top shelf of the cupboard. Novak grinned, moved behind Monica, and clung to her. Monica rammed her elbow into his abdomen, turned, and backhanded his groin. Novak gasped with surprise and some discomfort. He turned toward Devon and Vander.

"That's my girl," Novak gasped softly.

"Yeah, she wants you all right," Vander teased while snickering at his friend's discomfort.

Vander caressed Devon's hand then moved her hand onto his crotch. Devon immediately pulled her hand away with surprise and annoyance.

"Stop doing that!" she snapped.

"I'm sorry," Vander said gently and tensed with embarrassment. "With everything that's been going on around here, we haven't had much alone time."

Devon and Monica exchanged looks. And so continued their fictitious romance. The drugs couldn't wear off soon enough for Devon's comfort. It seemed odd that he was okay for nearly two hours though. Vander stood, moved behind Devon's chair, and affectionately massaged her shoulders.

"I can give you a nice, long massage," Vander suggested while grinning lustfully. "Maybe take our own bubble bath?"

She tensed and stopped Vander's hands on her shoulders. Although she actually enjoyed the sound of both the bubble bath and massage, she needed to put a stop to his unwitting behavior before it got out of hand.

"I really need to talk to Monica, you know, girl talk," she informed Vander.

Monica rolled her eyes.

Vander removed his hands from her shoulders and smiled politely. "We'll leave you to your girl talk and meet you in the lobby in fifteen minutes."

Vander kissed her quickly on the lips, startling her. Her heart skipped a beat in response. Devon stared after him as both men left the kitchen. Was it wrong that she actually enjoyed the kiss? She quickly dismissed all erotic thoughts from her mind. The last thing she needed was to join Vander in his delusions.

Monica snickered softly and hid her grin. "He's got a real bad case of the hornies," she teased.

"I'm glad you find it amusing," Devon scoffed and stood with disgust. "What am I supposed to do?"

"My advice--jump him."

She stared at Monica with surprise to her humorless joke. "I'm being serious."

"So am I," Monica replied casually. "Give the poor guy a thrill. I guarantee he'll roll over and sleep like a baby until the drugs to wear off."

"You want me to take advantage of a drugged federal agent?" Devon demanded.

"The drugs are only magnifying his feelings," Monica informed her. "You should be thankful everyone is mellow and horny rather than aggressive and violent. It could be a lot worse. We just need to make it until morning, and then they'll all return to their normal, boring selves."

"Well, not that I don't appreciate your expert advice, but I have no intention on sleeping with him."

"Who said anything about sleeping?" Monica teased and grinned lustfully at the thought.

"Monica--" Devon scolded.

"You're no fun," she quipped.

Devon glared her disapproval at Monica's comment then came at her with her own clever comeback. "I don't see you jumping Novak," she remarked firmly. "Where's *your* sense of fun? Why don't you take your own advice and give him a thrill?"

"Novak is a fruit loop jacked up on caffeine with a badge and gun," Monica grumbled.

"So what's the problem?" Devon remarked while smirking. "I'm sure he'd let you handcuff him to the bed."

Monica glared at Devon and appeared moderately offended by the bondage crack. "Are you seriously suggesting I'm into handcuffs and tying men to beds?"

"Well--"

"That's completely beside the point!"

Devon stared at her a moment with surprise then laughed softly. Monica snorted then laughed with her. There was nothing about her newly found friend that would surprise Devon. She'd never met a woman quite like Monica. She certainly wished she had some of her spirit. Unfortunately, the only spirit Devon had were those floating around and bringing chaos into her life. Ravin entered the kitchen from the backstairs and approached the refrigerator without interrupting their conversation. He removed a bottle of water and leaned on the counter at the far end.

Monica studied him a moment in silence then grinned lustfully. "How was your bubble bath?"

"Sudsy," Ravin casually replied.

Monica leaned across the counter closer to Devon. She muttered softly, "Twenty bucks says that's his actual personality. High IQ, low self-esteem, and scary calm. He's so tight; he won't even allow himself to trip."

Devon hid her smile then glanced at Ravin. She was still getting nothing from him. It had to be the drugs that kept his emotions from her. "Ravin?" she said while studying him.

He looked innocently at her. "Hmm?"

"How are you feeling?" she asked gently.

"Pretty good. I just got laid," he casually replied and sipped his water.

Devon hid her embarrassed smile and glanced at Monica, who bit her lip to keep from laughing. Monica was enjoying herself a little too much at the expense of those seemingly flying high on ecstasy. For one fleeting moment, Devon wondered what behavior Monica would display had she been exposed to the same drugs. On second thought, she didn't want to know.

Monica grinned at Devon. "Another twenty says he's never said those words to a woman before in his life."

Chapter Twenty-one

*D*evon, Monica, and Ravin walked along the grand hallway toward the lobby to meet with Novak and Vander. It was getting late, so Ravin offered Monica a room. After mercilessly torturing Devon for several minutes, Monica finally agreed to let her stay in her room. Vander couldn't object, since he was the one who insisted that no one stay alone in a room. She knew she couldn't stay in the same room with Vander and Novak in their hormone-induced condition, and spending some time alone with Monica sounded good to Devon. She was an interesting woman and her vibes all indicated she had little to hide emotionally or otherwise. She was the big sister Devon always wanted. Screams were heard coming from the game room, startling all three. Vander, Novak, and Tyson appeared from the lobby, apparently alerted by the screaming as well. All six ran into the game room.

Sonya sat on the floor against the wall in only her undergarments. She appeared frightened while attempting to conceal her partially naked body. Harris was frantically zipping his pants as

Tyson approached. Her brother's look was wildly unpredictable as he stopped before Harris.

"What did you do to my sister?" Tyson demanded in a threatening tone.

"Nothing, I swear," Harris proclaimed while appearing flustered. "We were just fooling around!"

Tyson punched Harris in the mouth and sent him flying against the pool table. Harris was dazed but quickly moved to avoid Tyson, who came at him with a second swing. He darted around the pool table and held his hands up defensively.

"I swear, she came on to me," Harris proclaimed with alarm. "She just freaked for no reason!"

"You ain't in the city, rich boy," Tyson snapped. "That don't float here!"

"Let's just take it easy," Novak announced and attempted to calm the situation.

Vander slowly approached Sonya, who still appeared terrified, and lowered himself to one knee before her on the floor. He looked into her eyes and spoke in a soothing tone. "What happened, Sonya?" he asked gently.

She clung to her body and trembled while looking past him at nothing in particular. "It--it was a ghost," Sonya gasped. She finally looked at Vander, her eyes wide with fright. "His face was ripped apart, and he was covered in blood."

"I told you I didn't do anything!" Harris lashed out, regaining some confidence.

Novak looked at Harris and seemed curious. "Did you see this ghost too?"

Harris fumbled slightly and gently cleared his throat. "I was sort of *preoccupied*."

"Come on," Tyson said firmly to Sonya. "I'll take you to your room." He helped his sister to her feet, grabbed her clothing, and guided her from the room.

"We need to find this ghost and stop it," Novak proclaimed with all seriousness.

"How the hell do you intend to stop a ghost?" Vander demanded.

Devon couldn't believe two grown men, federal agents no less, were having this debate. Monica was having no part of it and quickly shared her disapproval with them.

"There are no ghosts," Monica launched back with a disgusted groan. "Get a grip, guys!"

"How do we stop their hallucinations?" Devon gently asked Monica.

She considered the question then groaned softly. "We need to stay calm and disprove what they're seeing," Monica informed her. "The last thing we need is for them to become agitated or aggressive."

"So we're supposed to go ghost hunting with them?" Devon suddenly asked.

"There's always plan B," Monica replied.

"What's plan B?"

"Distract them with a little cleavage."

Novak glanced toward the doorway, appeared stunned, and then quickly became agitated. "Son-of-a-bitch! That's the guy!" He ran past them and out the door.

"I guess we're ghost hunting," Monica said with a sigh then hurried after Novak.

Devon, Vander, and Ravin ran out of the game room after them. Monica took off after Novak and disappeared into the connecting hallway. Ravin followed them in less of a hurry. Vander took Devon's arm and immediately pulled her along the hallway toward the elevator.

"I need to take you somewhere safe," Vander said firmly while keeping a sturdy grip on her arm. "There's no telling who that lunatic is or what he'll do."

"Agent Hawk, none of this is real," she insisted and resisted the urge to pull away. She didn't want to agitate him further. "You need to calm down and think rationally."

Vander stopped her by the elevators and looked around with paranoia. "I am being rational," he announced. "I'm keeping you safe."

The elevator doors opened. Vander turned toward the open elevator as Tyson stepped out.

Tyson eyed Devon and smiled lustfully. "Were you looking for me, sexy?"

Vander suddenly pulled his gun from his shoulder holster and aimed it at Tyson. Tyson jumped with surprise and took a step back. Devon gasped with alarm as panic swept through her. Vander's look was serious and unpredictable, which frightened her. With how he was reacting, she didn't know if he'd feel justified pulling the trigger on the unarmed man.

"You just stay the hell away from her," Vander lashed out then forced Devon into the elevator.

Tyson was ready to jump in and save her when Devon stopped him.

"No, Tyson," she announced quickly, concerned for his safety. "I have this. It's okay."

Vander kept his gun aimed at Tyson and pushed the button. Tyson watched with a look of helplessness as the door closed, allowing Vander to take her away.

Chapter Twenty-two

$\mathcal{V}$ander hurried Devon into his guestroom and bolted the door behind them. He stared at the door a long, concerning moment while keeping his gun firmly clutched and aimed at the door. His paranoia sent shockwaves through Devon's entire body. She could feel every emotion within him rippling through her. Devon stared at him with concern. His feelings of fear were overwhelming. She was almost certain he hadn't been that afraid in all his adult life. Devon had no idea what he would do next, or if he'd pull the trigger at something he thought he saw. He stared at the door for several minutes before finally relaxing and lowering the gun. Vander turned toward her, groaned softly, and pulled her into his arms in a tight embrace. He held her so firmly; it felt like a python squeezing the life from her.

"It's okay. You're safe now," he whispered softly in her ear. "I won't let anyone hurt you."

Devon remained motionless in his arms and appeared aware of the gun in his hand as it pressed against her back. She attempted to remain calm, but it was proving difficult.

"I'd feel better if you'd holster your weapon," she said softly in a shaken voice.

Vander pulled away from her with a strange look, glanced at the gun in his hand, and then replaced it to his shoulder holster. He offered a tiny smile and gently touched her face.

"Is that better?"

Devon slowly nodded, although she was still concerned with the entire situation. She didn't know how to relax him, and his current state of mind was frightening to her. He was a ticking time bomb of emotions. Anything at any given moment could set him off. Vander guided her to the nearby bed and kept her close as he sat with her. She hesitantly sat with him in hopes to keep him calm but there were other concerns building up inside her. He again pulled her against him and stared at the door with the same paranoid look. His shoulder holster pressed against her, making her uncomfortable. She didn't want him to know how frightened she was in fear it would add to his paranoia and possibly increase his need to protect her in an extreme manner. She knew he wasn't the type to lose his head. She'd gotten that vibe clearly from him on their first meeting, so this was foreign and frightening. If she could keep him calm, she was sure the paranoia would decrease, perhaps even returning him to something resembling his old self.

"Your gun's pressing into me," she said timidly.

Vander was surprised, grimaced slightly, and removed his shoulder holster. Devon was relieved as he set it on the bed. She wanted his weapon as far from him as possible. There would be less chance of him accidentally shooting someone. He pulled her into his arms and attempted to comfort her. She wished his holding her did comfort her, but it made her less comfortable. Unfortunately, it relaxed him.

"Sorry--"

Devon attempted to relax in his arms to keep him calm, but she was worried about sudden mood swings. There was no telling what he might think he saw and what he might do about it when he did. It was strange how Sonya's hallucination was able to upset the balance of the entire room. Well, everyone except Ravin, who didn't react either way. It was some sort of mass hysteria brought on by Sonya's own hallucinations. She wasn't sure how long he held her there on the bed, but she could feel his emotions coming down from their roller coaster ride. There was only one fear that remained, in her opinion.

"What happened to us?" Vander asked softly while gently caressing her in his arms. "We used to be so close. Now you seem tense anytime I touch you." His seriousness was what frightened her most. "I can't even remember the last time we made love."

"I'm not surprised," Devon softly replied.

And that was her one concern remaining. She feared he'd swing the other way, and if she didn't shut it down, there was potential for his sexual desires to take over.

"Was it something I did?" he asked gently. "Something I didn't do?" He suddenly tensed and took a deep, alarmed breath. "Is there someone else?"

Devon was frightened by the comment and quickly met his serious gaze. "No, of course not," she quickly announced. She certainly didn't need him thinking she was cheating on him in their pretend relationship. That could come with dire consequences. "We've been under a lot of stress with all that's happened around here. Surely you understand that." She hesitated and considered her words carefully. "I'm grateful that you've been here for me."

Vander looked into her eyes and gently caressed her face. "I've missed you."

He kissed her warmly but passionately on the lips. Devon immediately tensed with surprise. He broke off the kiss but didn't move his mouth from hers.

"Please, Devon, just give me another chance," he begged softly. "That's all I'm asking."

Vander resumed kissing her and gently lowered her to the bed, startling her. Devon braced her hands to his chest in an attempt to keep things from escalating. She wasn't sure what to do. If she protested, would his paranoia return? If she didn't protest, there was a good chance she'd never get him off her. He had been drugged, and she had to stop him from doing something they'd both regret later. She gently attempted to stop his roaming hands, but he was persistent. His hand firmly caressed her leg and pulled it alongside his hip, allowing him to maneuver his body between her legs. He continued to kiss her warmly despite her lack of reciprocation.

"Agent Hawk, don't do this," she said softly between his loving kisses.

"Stop calling me that," he said gently while kissing her warmly.

His hands continued to caresses her body without hesitation while his hips pressed against her. She gasped slightly from the firm although pleasant sensation. A small part of her wanted to give in to his sexual advances, but she knew that would be wrong.

"If you ever had any feelings for me, you'd give me one more chance," he whispered softly between loving kisses. "Whatever I did, I'll make it up to you. You know I love you."

To him, their relationship problems were real, and she felt sorry for what he thought she was doing to him. He warmly kissed her neck and throat while running his hand firmly along her body despite her hands braced against his chest. Images of them making love flooded through her mind like a tidal wave. It was possibly the most powerful premonition she'd ever had. It was meant to happen. She'd foreseen it. She seldom saw visions of the future unless they were incredibly strong. This was strong and resisting it meant nothing.

Devon groaned softly, shut her eyes, and relaxed her hands against his chest. Vander immediately seized her lack of protest as an invitation, molded his body to hers, and kissed her warmly on the mouth. Devon uncertainly returned the kiss and allowed his hands to caress her entire body. As she surrendered her body to him, a thousand images and thoughts flashed through her mind. There were too many even to keep track. She saw visions of his childhood, things from his past, but mostly things sexual in nature. Her head was swimming in visions she could no longer control. She finally cleared her mind and stopped any psychic energy from making its way in, but it also forced her to concentrate on the here and now. And the here and now was Vander making love to her.

Chapter Twenty-three

*I*t was later that night. The few remaining survivors had locked themselves into their rooms for the night in hopes to get a couple hours of sleep. They would need their rest before starting another day of terror and fright. Cody and Trent seemed to be the only ones crazy enough to still be up and about. The two men sat at the lounge bar with glasses of whiskey before them and a mostly empty bottle close by. Both men were intoxicated to the point of incoherence and joked with each other like old friends. Concerns for their safety or the current situation hadn't occurred to either after their fourth or fifth drink. For Trent, getting drunk was a coping mechanism. All his friends were dead except Harris, so having a few drinks seemed only natural. For Cody, drinking was a way of life. He was rarely ever seen without a drink in his hand.

"So Sonya's your daughter?" Trent asked with disbelief then grinned and shook his head.

Cody smirked and nodded.

"Wow," Trent muttered, "she's totally hot. I don't think I'd want a hot daughter. I'd go insane the first time she brought a boy home."

"Yeah, I was an insane father in the beginning. It's a natural reaction. I used to beat the boys off with a stick to defend my little girl's honor," Cody remarked then chuckled softly and sipped his drink. "Turns out her honor was in question long before I'd had a chance to defend it."

"That does it. If I ever have a daughter, I'm sending her to a convent until she's forty."

Cody chuckled then attempted to focus on the clock behind the bar. He groaned with disgust at the time. "It's late, and I'm wasted," he announced wearily. "I'm going to bed before I forget where my room is." He appeared to consider his own comment and glanced around. "I certainly don't want to pass out down here. May never wake up."

"I hear you, man," Trent muttered. He could barely sit up straight and nearly fell off his stool. "But you did say things have been quiet lately, right?"

"We haven't had any deaths inside the hotel since the initial manifestation," Cody announced. "Just those who attempt to leave seem to fall victim to the evil ghosts."

"Ghosts?" Trent asked. "Who said anything about ghosts? Agent Hawk said--"

"Agent Hawk has seen them too," Cody informed him sternly. "It just took a while for them to show themselves to him."

"Huh? Ghosts?" Trent muttered. "Who'd have thought?" He stood from his barstool and attempted to maintain his balance before releasing the bar. "You tip the bartender. I'll flag a cab."

Both men laughed. Trent stumbled to the doorway while Cody took the comment literally and placed some money on the bar. As Cody stood and turned away from the bar, he witnessed Trent stumbling backwards.

"Some guys just can't hold their liquor," Cody announced while chuckling.

Trent turned while clutching his bleeding throat. There was a deep gash across his neck bleeding profusely in a waterfall of blood, soaking the entire front of his shirt. Cody was horrified as Trent collapsed to the floor. Cody looked at the doorway, but there was no sign of Trent's attacker. He clutched the bar to keep from falling and stood frozen while watching the doorway. When it seemed as if the killer had taken off, Cody bolted for the door. He stumbled over the bar stool and both he and the stool fell to the floor with a crash.

Cody lie on the floor a moment, dazed, then groaned softly and attempted to move to his feet with some disorientation. As he moved to his hands and knees, a shadow loomed over him. He slowly looked up at the person standing over him. The large knife dripping blood was only inches from his face. Cody gasped with horror.

✝

*D*evon slept peacefully in Vander's guestroom with the covers over her naked body. She slowly woke, although she wasn't sure why, and looked across the dimly lit room. Vander slept reclined in the nearby chair wearing only his pants. Since his shoulder holster remained at the foot end of the bed, she assumed his reason for being in the chair had to do more with reality setting in than staying awake to protect her. As she silently watched him from where she lie, she had mixed feelings about what had happened between them just a few hours earlier. She didn't doubt he was already blaming himself, and making a big deal about it would just make things worse for both of them. If anyone was to blame, it was Monica. She was, after all, the one who planted the evil seed in Devon's mind. Conceiting to his sexual advances seemed the best way to curb his paranoia, and Monica had been right. Devon just wondered if the cost hadn't been too high. She didn't share Monica's relaxed views on sexual relationships. All she wanted to do now was avoid any and all conversation involving their romp. Pretending it didn't happen sounded appealing.

She silently leaned across the bed and grabbed Vander's discarded shirt, being the closest article of clothing she could find. She hastily slipped into his shirt. As she buttoned the shirt, his eyes opened. She glanced at him as he shifted uncomfortably in the chair.

"Can't you sleep?" she asked softly while buttoning the shirt with trembling hands.

He took a deep, shaken breath and sat forward, clasping his hands between his knees. "No, not really. I've been trying to rationalize what happened earlier," Vander said timidly and attempted to make eye contact. "How sorry I am can't begin to describe what I'm feeling."

She snorted a soft laugh while avoiding looking at him. "Yeah, you were a persistent little bastard," she teasingly remarked and climbed out of the bed.

"That was more than persistence," he said gently with a guilty look on his face. "I forced myself on you."

Despite her unwillingness to discuss what happened, she cast a glare at him. "Trust me, if you had forced yourself on me, I'd be handing you your privates in one of those zip lock baggies," she remarked casually.

"You aren't just saying that to make me feel better, are you? Because I remember a lot of protesting," he remarked while staring at her, possibly attempting to gauge her reaction.

She sighed deeply, folded her arms insecurely across her chest, and studied him. "No, I'm not just saying that. Everyone in this hotel had been drugged. You weren't responsible for your actions, but I was in control of mine," she informed him and straightened proudly. "I'm not mad at you. It wasn't your fault, and you don't need to apologize."

"When a woman tells a man he doesn't need to apologize, that usually means he needs to apologize."

"If I accept your apology, can we drop it?"

"I'd be grateful if we did."

"Fine, apology accepted," she announced then studied him. "Are you back to your old self then?"

"I think so, although I've felt better."

"You should try to get some sleep. I'm going to take a shower."

Vander smiled gently and nodded. He moved onto the edge of the bed and studied her a moment in silence. "Thanks for looking out for me."

"Don't get all sentimental, Agent Hawk," she said. "We're all just trying to survive the same nightmare." She headed into the bathroom, closing the door behind her.

Vander pulled back the covers, looked at the bed, and appeared alarmed. He hurried to the bathroom and promptly knocked on the door. Devon opened the door with a disgusted groan and glared at him. His look was serious.

"Tell me you weren't a virgin."

"Don't be ridiculous," she snapped despite the heat she felt rising in her cheeks.

He stared at her with disbelief. "I can't believe you weren't going to tell me and act like it wasn't a big deal."

"I stand by my decision, and I'm fine with it," she announced firmly. Her firm tone would have carried more weight if she hadn't felt the redness in her cheeks. She hated being called on his discovery. She hated that he knew.

"You're not fine with it, I can tell."

"Let it go, Agent Hawk, before you piss me off." Devon shut the door with surprising force.

†

*N*ovak lie naked beneath the covers as sunlight poked through the part in the curtains. Both he and the bed were severely rumpled from whatever had happened last night. An earthquake wasn't entirely out of the question. He slowly woke and groaned while holding his head as he fell onto his back. Novak panted a moment and seemed unable to move. The aftershocks weren't helping either.

"What the hell--?"

The curtains were pulled open. He looked toward the sunlight flooding into the room through the window and shielded his eyes. Monica had just finished opening the curtains where she stood alongside the window wearing only a tank top and panties. Novak stared at her with confusion then apprehensively eyed his naked body beneath the sheets. It was taking him a little longer to catch on than usual.

"Back from your trip?" Monica asked while raising a cocky brow. "I should warn you, you're going to feel like shit the rest of the day."

Her grin mocked him as she walked past him, entered the bathroom, and shut the door behind her. Novak slowly sat up and stared at the bathroom door with a bewildered look. He lifted the sheets, glanced at his naked body, and then looked back at the bathroom.

"What the hell?" He remained puzzled then groaned softly as if finally putting it altogether. "Please let me remember what happened last night."

The shower was heard running within the bathroom. Novak looked at the closed bathroom door, strummed his fingers on the bed while deep in thought, and then suddenly grinned.

"Yeah, shower sex," he announced cheerfully. "If you can't remember the night before, there's always round two in the morning."

Novak jumped from the bed, despite his unsteadiness, and streaked across the bedroom in his birthday suit. He grinned boyishly and gently knocked on the door.

"Is there room for two?"

"Don't even think about it!" Monica snarled through the door in response.

Novak appeared stunned while staring at the door then sank into thought. "Okay, that's not a good sign," he muttered softly. His eyes suddenly widened in horror. "Oh, God," he gasped, "I hope I didn't misfire."

Novak chewed on his fingernail and returned to the bed while deep in thought.

Chapter Twenty-four

*R*avin stood by the window and stared out into the bright, sunny morning. It was a beautiful day for early spring. It didn't seem possible that things could be so dismal on such a beautiful day, but life was filled with cold, cruel irony. Gemma shuffled out of the bedroom wearing a plush, white signature hotel bathrobe. She looked rumpled and severely hung over almost as if she'd spent several days drunk out of her mind. She collapsed onto the corner of the sofa and groaned softly while holding her head. Ravin didn't look at her. He couldn't look at her.

"What the hell happened?" she muttered softly.

"We were all drugged for the last three days," he reported gently.

She didn't seem surprised by the comment. Somewhere inside, she must have remembered hearing about being drugged. She stared off as if in a trance. "The last thing I remember was all those people in the dining room--"

Ravin slowly turned and looked at her with a stunned expression. "Are you serious?" he asked. "You don't remember anything after the dining room?"

She sank into thought, considered his comment, and shook her head. "A thousand images are flashing through my mind, but I don't know what they mean. Sort of like a bad porn movie on an endless loop."

Ravin tensed, inhaled a deep, shaken breath, and timidly approached her. He sat on the arm of the nearby chair and seemed extremely uncomfortable. He had a difficult time looking at her, which wasn't surprising.

"I've been trying to figure out what to say to you," he said gently. "I wanted to lie and tell you I didn't remember anything that happened, but I remember all of it--every insane detail."

She sheepishly glanced at him and fidgeted. "We slept together, didn't we?"

"That's putting it mildly," he muttered softly and again avoided looking at her.

Gemma closed her eyes, held her head, and groaned softly. "That would explain why you were in the endless loop of porn movies."

He attempted to remain strong but his insecurities seeped through. "Neither of us were responsible for what happened," Ravin gently informed her, "but that doesn't mean I don't feel terrible for my aggressive behavior."

Gemma suddenly chuckled. "From the bits and pieces I'm remembering, I was the aggressor," she casually informed him without looking up.

Ravin shifted uncomfortably on the arm of the chair. "Maybe so, but I'm rather ashamed of a lot of what I did," he announced then appeared to recall something that caused him to shutter. "One incident in particular has me a little *disturbed*."

She cast a glance at him, allowing her eyes to stray to the scratches on his neck. "You mean when I freaked out and scratched you?"

He looked away shamefully. "I was hoping you wouldn't remember that."

"I don't blame you," she said gently. "I went a little crazy and tried to hurt you for no reason. You had to stop me from beating you."

"It still bothers me," he said gently.

Gemma shifted on the sofa and finally looked at him. "It's okay, really."

He stared at her a moment in uncomfortable silence then inhaled deeply before speaking. "I promise no one will ever hear about our indiscretions from me."

A strange smile crossed her face as she laughed. "I think everyone already knows." She stared at him with a serious look. "I'm okay with what happened, Ravin," she said timidly. "I actually enjoyed every *insane moment.*"

His expression suddenly dropped as he stared into her eyes with surprise. "Really?"

Gemma smiled timidly and nodded. "Yes, really," she replied softly. "If I were going to have a wild, three-day fling, I'm glad it was with you."

There was an odd silence between them. Ravin shifted on the arm of the chair while staring at her. There was something more on his mind, but he was reluctant to say it aloud.

"What if I didn't want it to end?" he asked gently.

A tiny smile crossed her weary face. "I'd be very happy to hear that."

Ravin stared at her a moment then moved closer and uncertainly kissed her on the lips. Gemma immediately returned the kiss and pulled him onto the sofa with her.

†

*D*ino crouched before the large bloodstain on the floor in the lounge and studied it. He was deep in thought, and the look on his face conveyed his concerns. Vander passed by the lounge then doubled back and entered. He saw Dino examining the blood just within the doorway, appeared concerned, and quickly approached. He studied the area on the floor near where Dino crouched. By the large amount of blood, the outcome of what must have happened was obvious. Dino had to have known Vander was standing over him, but he didn't bother looking back at him.

"What happened?" Vander asked then looked around for signs of a body.

"I don't know, but that's a lot of blood," Dino said then indicated the bar. "There's more over there too. Something bad happened last night." Dino straightened and eyed Vander with a stern, serious look. "My brother is missing."

Vander looked over the bloodstain then approached the neatly placed chairs and looked at the smaller bloodstain by the bar. He glanced back at Dino, who now approached the bar as well.

"Is anyone else missing?" Vander asked.

"It's too early to tell," Dino replied with a defeated sigh while nervously looking around. He suddenly seemed annoyed and shook his head with disgust. "I told him a hundred times about his drinking--"

"With the drugs starting to wear off, I wouldn't expect anyone to be up early," Vander announced. "We'll need to see who's missing."

Vander examined the room for any indications of a struggle, although nothing seemed out of place. Whatever had happened seemed to be quick and without altercation, as with the other deaths. The entire situation was disturbing on several levels.

Dino stared at Vander with a look of surprise. "Drugs?" he suddenly questioned. "I hadn't heard anything about drugs. You mean the ghosts weren't--"

"Not real," Vander informed him.

"I don't get it. Why drug us?" Dino suddenly asked. "If that was the intention, why not just kill us all? Obviously whoever is behind this had the means and plenty of opportunity."

"That's just part of the puzzle," Vander replied while glancing at the two glasses on the bar. "Can you account for your people while I account for mine?"

"Yes, of course."

"Two scotch glasses and two bloodstains," Vander announced with a defeated sigh while looking around. "Any idea who was in here drinking last night?"

"Cody was the only one with access to the scotch," Dino replied and indicated the empty bottle on the bar. "He'd found two bottles stashed in the kitchen our first night here." He shook his head with disgust. "Something's happened to him, I know it. That idiot has been making bad decisions his entire life, and now it looks as if he finally paid for it."

"Drinking out in the open with everything that's been going on around here wasn't exactly wise, but the drugs didn't help anyone keep a clear head either," Vander said then considered. "There's blood but no bodies. That's not the killer's style. He seems to prefer leaving his victims in plain sight, I'm guessing for dramatic effect. What would his reason be for moving the bodies in this instance?" He considered his own comment. "It's possible whoever was attacked managed to get away. I'll check for a trail of blood and then have a look around the infirmary."

Dino snorted a soft laugh and attempted a smile. "I appreciate your attempt at making me feel better, but I think we both know my brother is dead."

"It's not an attempt to make you feel better," Vander insisted. "The second bloodstain indicates minimal blood loss. Whoever was here at the bar has a fighting chance of being alive. We need to concentrate on finding out what happened to him."

Dino stared at Vander and nodded with conviction. "You're right," he announced. "I'll gather the others."

Chapter Twenty-five

Everyone remaining within the hotel that Dino and Vander could find had assembled in the lobby for a briefing on their situation. Felicia, Trent, and Cody were the only ones neither man could locate. Mostly everyone looked exhausted and hung over from their drug-induced bender. Although alarming, the news of potentially new victims wasn't surprising to anyone. Sadly, it was becoming just another tragedy, which with they'd need to confront.

"I think the last time I saw Felicia, she was in the dining room talking to the dead people," Ravin informed Vander from his seated position on the sofa alongside Gemma. "You'll have to forgive me; I'm a little fuzzy on details at the moment."

"Yes, she was there," Devon agreed then looked at Ravin on the sofa. "I was with you, don't you remember?"

He looked at her and took a moment to consider the question. "I suppose it could have been you." Ravin again looked puzzled. "At the time, I was convinced it was Rita Hayworth."

"My father and Trent could be passed out somewhere," Tyson informed them. "It wouldn't be the first time he didn't make it to his room after a night of drinking. Just because they were in the lounge--"

"What the hell was he doing drinking like that in the first place?" Dino demanded while glaring at his nephew. "If you knew he was there, why didn't you say something to him? Or at least come find me?"

"Since when am I responsible for my father's drinking?" Tyson snapped hotly. "At least I don't encourage his behavior by tying one on with him!"

"The situation here is a little different," Dino launched back at his nephew.

"You're not helping, Uncle Dino," Sonya said softly while holding her head.

"Family is supposed to look out for one another," Dino growled at Sonya then glared at Tyson. "What sort of kids let their father get drunk in a life or death situation?"

"Okay," Vander announced sternly. "That's enough of the finger-pointing for one morning. We're all a little on edge after everything that's happened the last few days. Let's just try to remain civilized and keep our heads."

Harris paced the length of the lobby before the large windows. "When are we going to get the hell out of here?" he impatiently demanded.

Vander was about to respond to Harris' question but Dino beat him to it.

"Someone will see the accident by the bridge and check on us," Dino informed them. "It won't be long now, I promise. We just need to stay put a little while longer."

"What makes you so sure help will make it here?" Harris demanded while glaring at Dino. "Your big plan is to sit and wait for help to arrive, but look what happened to every single person who attempted to leave this place. What makes you think a rescue will get through if we can't get out?"

"I made it to the ravine twice," Monica informed them from where she sat on a coffee table near the fireplace. "Help will arrive. As added insurance, I left a message with a warning on the rear window of the bus. Whoever comes along will see it and know there's trouble."

"Tomorrow is Monday," Tyson said. "Someone is sure to drive down that main road where you said that first car was stranded. They'll see the abandoned car in the middle of the road and search the road to town. They'll see the wrecked cars by the bridge, find the bodies, and bring additional help. Real help. The kind that carries automatic weapons, if we're lucky."

Gemma clung to Ravin's arm while they sat huddled together on the sofa. "This might be a good time to lock ourselves in our rooms," she announced.

"Safety in numbers," Novak replied.

Tyson glared at Novak and chuckled. "That didn't work out so well in the lounge or the pool area," he reminded him then considered. "Or on the bus or in the sunroom."

"Those people were all heavily drugged and then systematically murdered," Vander announced. "I can't say for certain how they were drugged, but they didn't kill themselves. Someone did it for them."

"I found some strange canisters in the kitchen. I could be mistaken, but I believe they contained knock out mist," Monica said to Vander. "Simply roll a canister into a room of unsuspecting people and, poof, everyone goes nighty night. They weren't nearly as sophisticated as what I'd seen in the Army." She shook her head defiantly. "There was no mass suicide, and it also explains why they didn't struggle against their attacker."

"So one of us is a killer?" Harris gasped and quickly looked around the room.

"Okay, let's not start pointing fingers at the person next to us," Vander announced sternly. "The killer could easily be someone we think is already dead. There's no telling who's unaccounted for, so let's try to stay calm."

"Although, we can account for those who are already dead," Tyson remarked. "It won't be pleasant though."

Sonya looked at her brother and appeared alarmed. "You mean a body count?" She gasped with horror then cringed. "That's disturbing."

While the others discussed the possibility of a body count, Ravin stood from the sofa and left Gemma's side. He headed behind the front desk and removed a small stack of paper, a clipboard, and a pen. Devon joined him by the front desk and studied him. His behavior seemed unchanged despite the drugs wearing off, and it had her curious. To her added perception, his personality hadn't changed at all. She still couldn't read him.

"How are you feeling?" she asked gently.

"Rather well, considering," Ravin replied.

"It looks as though things between you and Gemma seem to have worked themselves out," she remarked.

"Surprisingly, yes," he replied and glanced at Gemma on the sofa across the room. She was caught watching him then looked away while smiling. Ravin looked back at Devon. "Turns out she's always liked me, but she was afraid to say anything because I was her boss." He hesitated and chuckled softly. "Her emotionally guarded boss." He then gave a nod at Vander across the room. "What about Agent Hawk's delusion of you being his girlfriend? There seems to be a lot of tension between the two of you."

"He's very uncomfortable around me right now," she reported gently.

"The way you've been eying him, I'm assuming something happened," Ravin said.

"It's nothing."

"You mean it's none of my business," he announced casually and hid his smile.

She took a deep breath and tensed. "He went over the edge last night after that incident in the game room and was hell bent on protecting me from the 'imaginary forces of evil'," Devon informed him. "I was concerned he'd hurt someone or himself, so I--" She fidgeted.

Ravin raised his brows in question then replied, "--took one for the team?"

She sighed deeply and insecurely rubbed her arms. "Yeah, I took one for the team."

✝

*T*he nearly seventy decomposing men and women in the dining room were still propped in chairs before the dining tables. It was gruesome and chilling to see them arranged as if they were having some sort of sick, undead party. Felicia's reasoning for doing something so macabre even while drugged seemed unfathomable. Sonya, Gemma, and Harris walked along the tables and glanced over the decomposing bodies while attempting to keep from breathing the foul stench of decay. Harris carried a clipboard while following the women and grimaced his distaste.

"This has to be one of the more disgusting things I've done in my life," Harris muttered.

"Did Ravin say Felicia arranged the bodies?" Sonya asked with disbelief.

"She wasn't in her right mind," Gemma announced and grimaced while looking at one of the decayed women. "We all went a little crazy in our own, special way."

Sonya frowned then laughed softly. "From the bits and pieces coming back to me, I'm going to agree with that. I can't believe I did some of what I think I may have done."

"You and me both," Gemma reported.

"You mean hooking up with Ravin?" Sonya asked and looked curious.

"That would be a polite way of putting it," Gemma replied and glanced at another table of dead men and women. "I consider myself lucky we sought each other out. With the way I was behaving--" Gemma took a deep breath and shuttered. "Despite it all, he kept a level head. He's probably the only reason I'm still alive. I honestly believe he kept me safe."

"Yeah, Tyson was pretty levelheaded for the most part too," Sonya remarked. "I'm lucky to have such a caring brother." She looked at Gemma with wide eyes. "Please don't ever tell him I said that."

"I'm sorry for not caring," Harris casually informed them. "Could you possibly save this little soap opera for a time when we're not knee-deep in rotting corpses?"

Both women looked at Harris with surprise then appeared embarrassed.

Chapter Twenty-six

Tyson, Ravin, and Monica walked along the well-worn path through the woods in the direction of the trees where the bodies still hung. Monica carried the bloodstained baseball bat clutched firmly in her hand. She looked like a woman with a mission, a very dangerous woman with a mission. All three stopped and stared at the men still hanging from the trees. They grimaced simultaneously at the sight. Despite having seen it before, it didn't have any less of an impact, especially considering the amount of decomposition with each passing hour. Tyson shook his head with disgust.

"It's so disrespectful to just leave them hanging like that," Tyson scoffed. "These people were my friends and neighbors. They shouldn't be left hanging like that."

"The less we disturb the crime scene--" Ravin began but was swiftly interrupted.

"Yeah, yeah, I know," Tyson muttered under his breath. "It's still disrespectful."

Ravin suddenly tensed while staring at the trees. Trent's lifeless, gutted body was hanging from one of the nearby trees not far from the others.

"Oh, God, I found Trent," Ravin said softly.

Monica and Tyson looked at the fresh corpse hanging by its neck. Monica frowned then shook her head. Tyson quickly looked around with concern.

"What about my father?" he suddenly asked.

Ravin looked as well. "No, I don't see him," he replied then looked at Tyson with some sympathy. "Maybe he wasn't with Trent in the lounge when it happened."

"There were two bloodstains in the lounge," Tyson insisted. "They were drinking together. I saw them. He has to be here."

"If he is," Monica gently informed him, "that's probably not something you want to see. Why don't you let us have a look around first?"

Tyson looked at one of the trees, groaned softly, and frowned with disgust. "Ah, son-of-a-bitch!"

Monica and Ravin looked at the nearby tree expecting to see Cody. Instead of Cody, they saw Darlene in the same condition as the others.

"If I had known this would've happened to her, I never would've let her go off like that," Tyson remarked. His sadness quickly turned to anger. "I don't get it. She was riding away from town." He looked at the others. "The girl was riding fast. How could this have happened to her? How did the bastard get her?"

"That's a good question," Monica announced. "Either you or Agent Hawk would have heard a rifle firing from a great distance after she rode off, so she couldn't have been shot."

"What about an arrow?" Ravin asked. "Do people still hunt with those?"

"Not much around here anymore," Tyson replied. "They used to years ago. I'm sure someone has one, but our killer wouldn't have known she was going for her friend's horse. That was decided last minute while we were already out in the woods." He shook his head with disbelief. "The killer couldn't be psychic, and he certainly wouldn't have been carrying a bow and arrow concealed in his pocket."

Ravin looked around and appeared concerned. "Maybe the killer was in the woods the entire time."

"You mean patrolling the area and watching us coming and going from the hotel?" Monica asked then looked around. "Like he's hunting us?"

"It had to be an ambush," Tyson announced. "Someone's hiding out there just waiting to pick us off."

A faint, strange sound caught Monica's attention. She apprehensively looked around in an attempt to pinpoint its location. The other two didn't seem to notice anything and became alarmed to her sudden alertness.

"Did you hear that?" she whispered.

Ravin and Tyson quickly looked around the area, scanning for any sign of would-be killers. One of the bodies separated from its head with a hideous ripping sound and fell to the ground with a dull thud. All three grimaced.

"I wish I hadn't seen that," Tyson grumbled.

There was movement within the woods, alerting all three and spreading fear through them. It was the sound Monica had originally heard.

"I heard that," Ravin gasped softly.

Whatever the sound, it was bigger than a dog. The rustling within the woods alarmed all three as it got closer.

"It sounds big," Tyson responded while quickly scanning the woods.

All three moved closer together with their backs to one another and kept watch in every direction surrounding them. Monica clutched the baseball bat and prepared to fight whatever came at them. The rustling grew louder not far from the bodies near some thick brush. All three spun in the direction of the sound and stared with anticipation. The saddled horse appeared from the woods and hobbled onto the path. The reins were tangled around its front legs, limiting its mobility. Monica lowered the bat while groaning softly. Ravin and Tyson exhaled softly.

Tyson snorted an uneasy laugh and raked trembling fingers through his hair. "I damned near shit my pants."

Monica ignored Tyson's comment and slowly approached the horse, so she wouldn't frighten it.

"Oh, you poor thing," she said sweetly to the horse.

The horse greeted her without hesitation and snickered its pleasant reply. She patted the horse's neck then gently untangled the reins from its legs. Once she had the horse free from its reins, she checked the saddle and tightened the girth. Both men watched her with curious looks.

"What are you doing?" Tyson asked.

Monica placed the reins over the horse's neck and looked at Tyson with a cocky expression. "What does it look like I'm doing?" She swiftly mounted the horse without releasing her baseball bat and situated herself in the saddle. "I'm heading out to the main road and see if I can get a cell phone signal or flag down some help," she informed them.

Tyson indicated Darlene's body, gutted and hanging from the nearby tree. "That was Darlene's big plan too," he scoffed, "and look what it got her. You don't know what's out there."

"There are no monsters out here, and it wasn't ghosts who killed these people," Monica growled with irritation. "Since you never heard a rifle being fired and no one has been shot, I'm going to assume our killer doesn't have a gun, which gives me the upper hand."

"How do you figure?" Tyson asked.

"Because," she snapped in response, "that makes me the more dangerous predator. Now get out of my way or I'll run your ass over."

Tyson was surprised by her tone and quickly stepped out of her path. "Yes, ma'am."

Ravin joined Tyson on the edge of the path as Monica sent the horse into a slow canter and rode past them with her baseball bat casually reclined across the saddle in front of her. Both watched her ride toward town with all the confidence of an entire Marine platoon. Ravin slowly shook his head while staring after her as his mouth hung open.

"That's one scary woman," Ravin muttered.

"Yeah, she's kind of hot."

Ravin's brows knitted as he turned his head and glared at Tyson. Tyson chuckled softly and slapped Ravin on the chest.

"We have work to do," Tyson announced and indicated the bodies. "Let's take roll call and get the hell out of here before someone does the same to us."

Chapter Twenty-seven

Vander and Novak leaned against the wall within the spa just outside the ladies' restroom while waiting for Devon. Both men were lost in their own little worlds and were awkwardly silent. Novak finally straightened, tensed, and looked at his friend.

"Let me ask you something," Novak suddenly said in a firm and serious tone. "If you were drunk or, oh, let's say unwillingly drugged, and you'd spent the night with a woman. What would it mean if the next morning she acted like you barely existed?"

"I would assume it meant you'd slept with Monica," Vander announced then gave him a puzzled look, "but I thought she couldn't stand the sight of you."

"I know, right?" Novak blurted out and vigorously shook his head. "Something definitely happened. I know we had to have slept together last night, but then she blows me off--and not in the way I would have liked." He was now unable to stand still. "I mean, I'm usually pretty dynamic in the bedroom, so I don't understand her behavior."

"I think it's pretty simple," Vander replied. "She got what she wanted, left money on the dresser, and slipped out while you were asleep."

Novak sneered at him.

Devon appeared from the bathroom and casually walked past them. "Or maybe you didn't satisfy her."

Both men suddenly looked at her as she passed and shared the same expression. "What's that supposed to mean?" both suddenly demanded.

Novak glared his disapproval at Vander. "Why are you so defensive?" he demanded. "I'm the one she insulted."

Both men followed her, hounding her like defensive, little boys. She didn't bother looking back at either.

"I assure you, that's not the case," Novak informed her while keeping stride. "I've never been a one-hit wonder in my life." He seemed a little too proud of the fact and wasn't about to let it go. "Every woman I've ever been with has *always* come back for a repeat performance."

Devon pushed open the steam room door and peered inside. It was empty. She continued through the spa without looking at him and showed little interest in the conversation.

"No offense, but I think she's more into the big, tough, burly Marine type," Devon replied dryly.

"If I'm not manly enough for her, then why did she sleep with me in the first place, Miss Smarty-pants?" Novak demanded while directly on her heels.

Devon shrugged. "Scratching an itch?" she suggested without care.

Novak glared at Vander and was annoyed. "I'm really starting to not like your girlfriend."

Devon suddenly stopped and spun around, staring at Vander with a horrified look. "You told him?"

Vander stared at Devon with the surprise evident on his face. His mouth slowly dropped open in an attempt to respond but no words came out.

Novak suddenly gasped and looked between the two. "No way! You two?" he suddenly demanded then glared at Vander and frowned. "You never tell me any of the good stuff."

"Nothing happened," Vander muttered, although it was obviously too late to play dumb.

Novak was humored. "Between her blushing and your guilty look, I'd say plenty happened," he said then grinned. "I think I'll check out the men's locker room. You two can check out the steam room." He raised his brows lustfully. "Take as long as you need. I'll wait."

Vander attempted to speak but Novak was already heading across the spa. Devon slowly shook her head and felt the color burning her cheeks.

"I am so sorry," she said softly. She felt like an idiot for having blurted that out. "I assumed you told--"

He stared at her with surprise and shook his head. "You honestly thought I'd brag about what happened? Give me some credit. I'm not some horny, teenage boy." He hesitated and then considered. "Or Novak."

Devon frowned as they continued to walk more slowly across the spa together. "I wish you'd stop acting so uncomfortable around me," she said gently.

"Maybe if you weren't so tense around me--"

Vander opened the women's locker room door, peered inside, and then entered. Devon followed him inside. They crossed the small locker room and approached a set of elegant, frosted shower stalls. Vander checked inside each of the stone shower stalls. When they found no one, they headed back toward the entrance.

"I'm only tense because you're so uncomfortable," she replied gently. "Why can't you just let it go?"

Vander paused by the locker room door and turned to face her. "I was a mutt in heat and you were a virgin. That's not something I can just let go. Just admit it bothers you. Get mad. Yell at me. Do something."

She stared at him a moment in silence then groaned with annoyance. "Fine, it bothers me."

He appeared surprised by her bluntness. "It does?"

"Yes, of course it does," she suddenly lashed out and stared at him with disbelief. He was being oddly dense for someone who felt so guilty. "Do you actually think I wanted my first time to be a one-night stand with some guy I barely know? How dense are you?" She took a deep breath and attempted to relax. "But it's not your fault that it bothers me. I made that decision. I let it happen. Can't we just forget it and go back to the way things were, Agent Hawk?"

"You want to pretend nothing happened?" he demanded with a look of surprise.

"Don't you?"

He vigorously shook his head without taking his eyes off her. "No, I don't. It happened, and I'm glad that it happened. I wanted you the moment I saw you at the fundraiser," Vander informed her possibly louder than he'd intended. "No matter what you think, we shared something special and passionate, so stop calling me Agent Hawk, it's insulting." His irritation was escalating. "And you might think last night was a one-night stand, but I doubt you'll be able to get rid of me that easily."

Devon stared at Vander with surprise. A thousand thoughts raced through her head. There were a hundred things she could say to him at that moment, but only one thing came to mind. She moved past him for the door. Vander frowned and looked away. Devon locked the door and turned to face him. She took a deep breath and stared into his eyes.

"Those showers looked very inviting," she announced.

Vander stared back at her with surprise then suddenly groaned. "You read my mind." He pulled her against him and kissed her passionately.

Chapter Twenty-eight

*N*early twenty minutes later, Vander and Devon exited the woman's locker room while affectionately clinging to each other. The general mood between them had changed, and both were more relaxed than they had been all day. Devon was glad they'd aired their differences over a hot shower together. Their hair was slightly wet and smiles were permanently chiseled on their faces. They stopped when they saw Novak leaning against the nearby wall with his arms folded across his chest and a disapproving look on his face. Devon immediately blushed and avoided looking Novak in the eyes. He shook his head with disgust.

"You take me far too literally," Novak snapped.

Vander attempted to conceal his boyish grin. "It's not how it looks."

Novak rolled his eyes and straightened. "Yeah, I'm sure it's not. If you two are finished screwing around, I'd like to get back to our search. We do have three missing people and a lot of ground to cover."

All three headed across the spa. The door was suddenly thrown open, alarming them. Novak and Vander had their guns drawn almost immediately to the sound of the door. Dino hurried into the spa and approached them. Something obviously had him bothered. Vander and Novak relaxed and replaced their guns to their shoulder holsters.

"I thought you'd like to know, they found Trent hanging in the woods with the others," Dino announced with disgust. "No sign of my brother or Felicia though." His irritation was evident by the look on his hard face. He wasn't holding it together as well as he had the last few days. "My nephew said that militant type woman took off on the horse toward the main road to find help. Stupid girl's going to get herself killed."

"Monica?" Novak asked.

"Yeah, that's the one," Dino replied with a soft snort. "I'm going to help the others in the pool area. I need to keep busy. If you see my brother, let me know."

All three nodded and watched Dino leave the spa in almost as much of a hurry as he had arrived. He looked like a man ready to explode on someone, and he wasn't the sort of man to get on his bad side.

Novak appeared concerned and looked at Vander. "Do you think she'll be okay?"

"Who? Monica?" Vander suddenly asked. He managed a soft laugh. "She'll survive longer than any of us."

"Maybe I should go after her."

"Alone?" Vander shook his head defiantly. "No, that's not a good idea. We still don't know what's out there."

"Our killer is a live person," Novak remarked. "I have my gun, and I'm willing to use it."

"And our live person killer could have a sniper buddy sitting out there just waiting to pick off anyone who leaves," Vander informed him.

"Exactly why I need to make sure Monica made it out okay," Novak informed him. "We're trained to handle this sort of situation, and I'm going to handle it."

"Novak--"

"I'll be back before dark," he insisted then turned and hurried from the spa before Vander could protest.

Vander stared after him with his mouth hanging open then shook his head with disgust. "I don't know which one is crazier," he remarked.

"They would make an interesting couple," Devon announced. "Providing they don't kill each other first."

Vander chuckled softly then guided Devon toward the spa door.

✝

All twelve dead bodies, which had been floating in the pool for the last few days, had been pulled from the water and were lined up along the indoor patio. They were severely bloated from the water and displayed their own, unique variation of decomposition. The pool water remained tinged pink from all the blood, maintaining its eerie effect. Gemma, Dino, and Sonya stared at the bodies with disbelief to their condition. Harris wrote on the clipboard and cringed several times while attempting not to look at the bloated bodies only a few feet away. The smell was a foul mixture of chlorine and decaying flesh, which quickly filled the entire room.

"That is gross," Harris muttered and cringed from the smell. "I can't believe I'm actually doing this willingly."

"They're almost unrecognizable," Dino replied while shaking his head. "They barely look human anymore."

"I recognize them; unfortunately," Gemma said softly while taking a deep, shaken breath.

"Me too," Sonya almost whispered and seemed unable to tear her eyes away from the gruesome, decaying bodies. "It's hard to believe these are the people I used to say good morning to the last two years."

Dino looked at Gemma and his niece. He appeared sympathetic, which was almost out of character for the hardened man. "After we're done here, why don't you ladies get cleaned up?" Dino said gently then cleared his throat and attempted to return the tough guy act. "This hasn't been easy on any of us, and after helping pull those bodies from the water--"

"I wouldn't mind washing up a little," Sonya said then looked at Gemma and smiled timidly. "We can grab some uniforms from the kitchen and shower in the spa. Maybe take a little soak in the hot tub."

Gemma fidgeted and hid her tiny smile. "I hate to admit it, but that does sound good," she replied timidly.

Harris looked at the bloated, dead bodies and frowned. "I think I'm going to avoid water," he announced then reconsidered, "--for the rest of my life."

"Just don't take too long," Dino informed both women. "Lock the door and keep alert. When you're finished, meet us in the lobby." His toughness quickly returned. "Just an hour, okay? No longer or I'll come and get you."

Both women nodded.

✝

*M*onica rode the stocky, black horse toward the older couple's once stranded car in the now barely flooded roadway. The water had almost completely receded over the last two days. There was a good chance she'd be able to start the car and drive to the nearest town. She dismounted the horse, tied it securely to a nearby tree, and approached the car with her baseball bat. She skillfully twirled the bat and held it in a threatening manner as she approached the driver's side door. She peered inside the car then attempted to open the door. It was locked.

"Unbelievable--"

Monica stared at the car only a moment before coiling back with the bat and smashing the driver's side window. As the glass shattered, the horse snorted while watching her. Monica cleared away the glass on the seat. The interior of the car had been severely flooded as well and a pool of water remained on the floor. Monica flopped onto the driver's seat and felt around beneath the wheel. She removed several wires and attempted to hotwire the car. There was a slight grinding sound. The car was possibly too flooded to run ever again. She cursed softly and got out of the car with disgust. As she contemplated her next move, she glanced toward the tree line. The horse was gone! She was momentarily horrified. Her horror was quickly replaced with determination and hostility. Monica clutched her baseball bat and cautiously scanned the area. It was possible she hadn't tied the horse properly, but it seemed unlikely. Nothing moved and there wasn't any sound; not even from the horse. She heard the sound of air parting. She glanced at the bat and appeared puzzled. A small dart stuck out of the bat. Monica's eyes widened with horror. She suddenly gasped and ran for the woods. Something stung her arm. She looked at the tiny dart embedded in her upper arm. Without slowing, she pulled the dart out and ran into the woods.

Monica ran for several minutes before appearing at the wreckage site. She suddenly stopped, held her head, and fell against one of the trees. The world was now spinning and it wouldn't be long before she was unconscious. With all her strength, she straightened and stumbled toward the wrecked cars. The sound of movement within the woods was getting closer, and she would soon be trapped. She looked at the ravine up ahead with the car sticking out of it. Monica clutched her baseball bat with a look of determination and stumbled for the ravine.

Chapter Twenty-nine

$\mathcal{G}$emma and Sonya soaked in the spa hot tub and were relaxed for the first time since the nightmare started. The spa was unusually quiet, although neither seemed to mind, and with the door locked, they felt fairly safe. The last few days had been exhausting, although neither remembered too many details beyond the dining room poisoning. Both just wanted to release some stress and feel somewhat human again.

"I always wanted to try the spa," Sonya informed Gemma, "but it was too expensive even with our employee discount."

"Ravin let those of us in the office use it after hours," Gemma informed her. "As long as we straightened up afterwards, he didn't care."

"Ravin, huh?" Sonya teased and flashed a lustful smile. "What happened to Mr. Waverly?"

Gemma groaned softly, rolled her eyes, and smiled timidly. "After three days of drug induced sex-capades, I think we're entitled to be on first name basis."

Sonya giggled softly then studied her and seemed curious. "How did you end up with Ravin?" She hesitated. "I mean, like me, you probably don't remember much about what happened, but it just seems a little odd. When everything went to hell, how did you two end up together?"

"I'm not entirely sure what happened," Gemma replied. "I remember freaking out on him in the wine cellar. I remember hitting him, and he just held me until I stopped. Next thing I know, we were going at it on the wine cellar floor. I still have no idea who initiated or how it even came about." She sank into thought and shook her head. A strange smile then crossed her face. "I can't even tell you how many times we went at it over the last three days. It's just a collage of sexual images one after another." Gemma chuckled and seemed almost humored. "It was pretty intense. I'm just glad all that wild sex didn't kill him."

"Well, it is the way all men want to go," Sonya teased but appeared uncomfortable by the conversation.

"I'm so sorry, Sonya" Gemma announced gently. "Am I making you uncomfortable with talk about sex with our boss? I didn't mean to--"

"No," Sonya quickly interjected. "No, it has nothing to do with you and Ravin. It's just, well, there's something about Ravin I think you should know."

Gemma was interested and possibly concerned by Sonya's tone. There was a strange noise that sounded like something metal rolling. Both women became alert, jumped out of the hot tub, and frantically slipped into the plush, spa robes while looking around. Nothing seemed out of place and nothing moved. Gemma looked at a large, rolling laundry bin toward the back of the spa. It moved slightly. Gemma gasped and grabbed Sonya's arm. She indicated the laundry bin. Both women stared at the bin a moment. Sonya nodded toward the main door. The laundry bin squeaked as it moved. Sonya and Gemma were about to turn and run when Felicia appeared from the large laundry bin. Both women screamed then relaxed to discover it was just Felicia. The poor, exhausted woman was visibly shaken while holding her head. Sonya and Gemma hurried toward her.

"Felicia, we've been looking for you," Sonya announced while looking over the laundry bin Felicia had obviously been passed out within.

"What happened?" Gemma asked as they helped her out of the large bin.

Felicia slowly shook her head. "I don't know. In the middle of the night, I woke up in the dining room with all the bodies. I've

151

never been so freaked out in my life. I thought I heard someone coming. Whether it was real or not, I panicked and ran." She nervously looked around. "It's all sort of hazy, but I remember hiding in the laundry bin. I guess I must have passed out or something."

"We need to take you to the lobby with the others," Gemma said. "Everyone was worried about you."

"Yeah, I'd be grateful," she replied. "What happened? Why do I feel like I'm hungover?"

"We were all drugged," Gemma informed her. "We still don't know who or why, but at least the drugs have worn off now. No more hallucinations."

"I have no idea how I even ended up in the dining room," Felicia informed them while holding her head. "Did I see correctly? Did someone position the bodies in the chairs at the tables?"

"Didn't you do that?" Gemma asked.

"Me? Are you kidding?" Felicia gasped. "I wouldn't do that, at least, I don't think I would do that. I'm not really sure what's real the last few days."

"Yeah, we're all kind of there," Sonya replied. "You'll feel better once you're with the others in the lobby."

Felicia remained disoriented. "Please tell me I didn't have sex with all those men."

"I don't know about all those men," Sonya replied, "but I can name at least three."

She groaned softly and held her head. "How will I ever be able to look them in the eyes again?"

Sonya was sympathetic while gently caressing Felicia's shoulder. "You don't have to worry about that, Felicia," she said gently. "None of them survived."

Gemma gave Sonya a strange, almost horrified stare to the comment meant to comfort Felicia. Felicia just blinked with her mouth hanging open while staring at Sonya. Gemma and Sonya slipped back into their borrowed waiters' uniforms while Felicia remained tense and paced near the spa door. As she stood with her back to the spa door, it slowly opened behind her. Felicia nervously turned toward the now opened door. A man in a cloak and mask stood in the doorway directly in front of her. She opened her mouth to scream. The killer struck her in the head with a hammer. She barely managed a scream as the killer struck her repeatedly and violently in the head, impaling her skull with each thrust. Gemma and Sonya turned to the sound and saw the gruesome attack and Felicia's blood painting the once white room each time the hammer was flung back. They screamed hysterically. Felicia's body finally collapsed to the floor, stopping the grisly assault. The killer briefly looked down at what remained of Felicia's head and face then looked at Gemma and Sonya. His sights were now on them. Gemma looked around then grabbed an ax from the nearby wall. Sonya pulled on her.

"Are you insane? Run, damn it," Sonya cried out.

Gemma and Sonya ran across the spa with the killer only a few feet behind them and gaining ground. They ran into the steam room. Sonya slammed and bolted the door just seconds before the killer slammed into it. Both women screamed, but he was unable to get in. The killer thrust his body against the door and attempted to break it open. The door didn't budge. The killer moved away from the window, allowing both women to exhale with relief. Gemma slowly approached the door and glanced through the small window to see if he'd gone. The hammer suddenly struck the window with a dull thud. Both women screamed. Gemma jumped backward and joined Sonya, who clung to her arm. The glass didn't break. After several attempts, the killer finally moved away from the window. Sonya and Gemma stared at the window, but neither felt confident enough to get close enough to look out. There was no sound, just eerie silence. There was a strange hissing sound that followed. Steam flooded the room, rolling in like a rogue fog. Both looked around with surprise and then alarm. The steam quickly engulfed them.

"It's okay," Sonya told Gemma while clinging to her arm. "It'll only reach a certain temperature. There's no way he can override it. He's just trying to trick us into thinking we'll cook in here."

"Are you sure?" Gemma asked while nervously clutching the ax that was already becoming wet from the steam.

"Absolutely," she replied. "Tyson said someone got stuck in here once. Dehydration is the only real threat, and that would take a while even at maximum temperature. We'll just wait him out. My Uncle Dino knows we're here."

Gemma didn't appear convinced but made an effort to relax. She set the ax aside. "So we wait--and sweat."

Chapter Thirty

*N*ovak climbed the ravine near the wrecked cars and looked around. The entire area was eerily silent and nothing moved. The site easily reminded one of a post-apocalyptic scene straight out of a horror movie. He removed his gun and cautiously walked through the wreckage then continued toward the party bus. The tinted windows kept the interior private, forcing him to enter the bus to search it. Novak slowly entered the bus with his gun clutched firmly in his hand. He suddenly stopped and stared with a look of horror on his face. All fourteen dead people were painstakingly positioned on the leather bench seats in seemingly natural positions. The killer had returned to the bus! As he looked toward the back of the bus, the rear emergency door was now partially open. Monica's message for help had been crudely expunged from the window. Novak stared at the dead men and women a moment longer then cautiously walked along the wide aisle toward the emergency door. He looked at each dead person as he passed. Some had their eyes open and seemed to stare at him. The deep gashes across their throats were gruesome and disturbing, leaving wide crevasses covered in dried blood. Despite the horrifying images, he couldn't look away.

A cell phone lie on the seat alongside one of the dead passengers with the screen still lit. Novak stared at the lit phone, uncertainly picked it up, and pressed a button. A picture of the dead people on the bus was revealed on the screen. Novak stared at the picture as terror and dread crossed his face. It almost certainly meant the killer had been on the bus just seconds before. Seconds? One of the dead men behind Novak lifted his head. Novak saw the man moving behind him through the glare on the cell phone screen. He dropped the cell phone and spun around with his gun aimed. Novak was suddenly struck on the side of the head. He fell into two of the bodies, dropping his gun, and all three crashed to the floor. Novak slowly moved to his hands and knees as his temple bled freely. The killer aimed a dart gun at his face. As the killer's finger tightened on the trigger, Novak punched him in the crotch. The killer fell to his knees and the dart gun flew across the aisle. Novak straightened on his knees and came face-to-face with Cody.

Without hesitation, Novak punched Cody in the face, sending him into the opposite side of seated bodies. Novak scrambled for the discarded dart gun, grabbed it, and aimed it at Cody. Cody tackled him, and both men rolled around the bus floor, struggling for control of the dart gun. Cody was now on top of Novak and attempted to aim the dart gun at his chest. Novak fired it before it could be used on him. The dart cracked the window with a distinct sound. Novak released the gun and punched Cody in the face. Cody was thrown backward, dropping the dart gun. Cody removed a Bowie knife from a leg strap and slashed at Novak. Novak leaped from the knife's path as it slashed his upper thigh. He scrambled to his feet while clutching his bleeding leg, darted from the party bus, and limped toward his SUV.

Cody leaped off the bus while replacing his cell phone to his pocket and ran after him. Novak opened the rear door, grabbed a tire iron, and turned just in time to deflect the Bowie knife. The knife sparked against the tire iron, slipped, and sliced Novak's forearm. Novak fell against the back of the SUV in agony as the tire iron fell from his hand. Cody stood over Novak, who clutched his bleeding forearm. Cody grinned most sinister and appeared to be enjoying himself.

"I can't wait until they find the bodies of you and your girlfriend together," Cody announced cheerfully, his face void of any sanity. "The two of you will be my masterpiece."

Novak's expression suddenly dropped. "Where is she?" he demanded. Despite his pain, he was now enraged. "What did you do to her?"

"She's around," he chuckled while mocking Novak with his evil grin. "Don't worry. The two of you will be together soon enough, I promise."

✝

*V*ander paced the lobby, looked out the window several times, and then looked at his watch with disgust. He'd been pacing for the last thirty minutes non-stop. Devon watched him pace in silence. Tyson entered the lobby with several pool sticks collected in his arms and set them on the coffee table.

"I found some weapons," Tyson announced then glanced at Vander, who continued to pace. He looked at Devon and indicated Vander with a nod. "Did his date stand him up?"

"He's waiting for Novak to return with Monica," she informed him.

"Monica's probably in the next county by now," Tyson muttered.

"I don't like this. He should have been back by now," Vander remarked while keeping close watch out the window.

"Maybe he hasn't found Monica yet," Devon announced. "Perhaps she decided to ride the entire distance to the next town. If he's stubborn enough to keep looking--"

"Yeah," Vander muttered, "he's stubborn enough."

Ravin hurried into the lobby and looked at the others. Something had him disturbed. "I can't find Gemma anywhere," he announced with fear in his eyes. "It's not like her to be gone this long."

"I thought she was with my Uncle Dino, Sonya, and that Harris character taking names," Tyson remarked. "Did you check the death rooms?"

"Yes, I did," Ravin retorted tersely and glared his displeasure, "and please don't call them that."

Vander turned to Devon with his own look of concern. "I can't just sit here," he informed her. "I have to find Novak before it gets dark."

"You can't go back out there," Tyson insisted. He shook his head in disbelief. "If something happened to him, what makes you think you'll survive?"

"He's my partner and my friend," Vander announced sternly. "I can't just let him fend for himself."

The thought of him going off on his own chilled Devon. "I'll go with you," she offered.

"Absolutely not," Vander announced sternly. "You're staying here, where it's safe--" He hesitated and reconsidered. "--safer."

Tyson groaned with a defeated sigh. "I'll go with you to find Agent Delano." He turned to Devon. "You can help Ravin find his little playmate."

Devon looked at Vander, uncertain what to do, and silently questioned him with her eyes.

"Stay with Ravin," Vander informed her with a reassuring nod. "I'll be back before dark."

Vander quickly kissed Devon, pulled away, and left before she could protest. Tyson grabbed one of the pool sticks they'd collected for weapons and hurried after Vander.

Chapter Thirty-one

Cody punched Novak in the abdomen then across the face. Novak fell against the Corolla with a loud thump. He was badly beaten and barely stood from the severity of his injuries. Cody straightened, grinned deviously, and took a picture of Novak with the cell phone.

"That's a keeper!" He replaced the cell phone to his jacket pocket, removed his Bowie knife, and moved closer to Novak. His psychotic grin mocked him. "I promise this will only sting for a second."

Cody moved the knife closer to Novak, prepared to slash his throat. A loud scream like a war cry was suddenly heard, startling both. The baseball bat struck Cody on the shoulder, throwing him sideways. Monica swayed while clutching the bloodstained baseball bat. She appeared disoriented and was barely able to focus, but the sinister look in her eyes was frightening all the same. Cody clutched his arm and the knife while staring at Monica with astonishment.

"How the hell are you still standing?" he demanded.

Monica swayed and attempted to focus on Cody while clinging to the bat. Her expression was cold and fixated. Her lack of response was chilling, but her labored breathing indicated she was in trouble and might soon pass out. Cody sneered and lunged at her with the knife. Monica cried out and swung the bat. She missed his head and struck the side window of the Corolla just near Novak, shattering the glass. The knife narrowly missed her. She swung in the opposite direction and struck Cody on the side of the head with a mild hit. He was tossed away from the car but quickly recovered. He turned toward her with the knife. Monica swung without aiming, struck Cody just under his arm, and knocked him to his knees. Before he could even react, Monica struck him across the face with the bat. Cody dropped to the ground and didn't move. Monica raised the bat above her head for another strike. Novak suddenly grabbed her around the waist and stopped her.

"Whoa! He's down! He's down!" Novak cried out with surprise to her hostility.

Monica swayed and attempted to relax while lowering the bat. Novak clutched both his bleeding leg and arm and fell against the Corolla. Without warning, Monica suddenly cried out and struck Cody's motionless body. She straightened and met Novak's stunned gaze.

"I prefer dead." Monica stared at Novak and attempted to focus. When she saw his injuries, her hostility turned to concern. "You're injured."

Novak removed his hand from his leg wound to reveal a large amount of blood. "Yeah, he got me good."

Monica removed her belt and tightened it securely around his thigh to control the bleeding. She straightened weakly and nearly fell over. "We need to get to the vet's office." She grabbed his arm, half leaned on him, and pulled him away from the ravine.

"Town is that way," he gently indicated while pointing toward the ravine.

Monica stopped with disorientation, turned while severely swaying, and pulled him toward the ravine. She dragged her bloody baseball bat listlessly behind her. Novak stared at her while clinging to his less serious arm injury.

"What did he do to you?" he asked.

She panted heavily while attempting to remain on her feet and see straight. "Tranquilizer dart," Monica muttered.

He appeared stunned. "How are you still standing?" Novak suddenly asked as they stopped before the car standing on end in the ravine.

She looked at him and attempted to focus. "Adrenaline," she gasped softly. There was the distinct possibility she didn't even see him despite staring directly at him. "You'd be surprised what your body can do after serving two tours in Iraq."

"You would have made one hell of an interrogator," Novak remarked.

She raised a brow while attempting to stare at him. "I did," Monica announced. "How do you think I learned to resist the effects of drugs?"

Novak clung to the remains of the car standing in the ravine while staring at Monica. "Okay, now I'm frightened."

✝

*S*onya and Gemma sat on the bench in the steam room as steam flooded the entire area, allowing for limited visibility. Both were drenched in sweat and looked exhausted from the heavy humidity. Gemma held the ax across her lap while both women rested their heads against the back wall. Sonya glanced at Gemma from where they listlessly sat.

"Do you think he's gone?" Sonya asked.

"I'm afraid to look."

Sonya slowly straightened and moved closer to the door. She peered through the small window and strained to look out through the steam. The hammer struck the shatterproof glass. Sonya let out a terrified scream and leaped back onto the bench alongside Gemma. She clung to her friend's arm.

"Definitely still there," Sonya gasped. She finally released Gemma and looked back at the door. "It's been an hour. Doesn't he have anything better to do?"

"I guess we're first on his 'to do' list," Gemma muttered and returned her head to the wall behind her.

"My uncle will come looking for us, I know he will," Sonya said while staring at the small window beyond the thick steam. "He knew where we were."

Gemma stood and paced the steam room with the ax securely in her hands. She suddenly seemed concerned. "We have to get out of here," she informed Sonya. "We can't wait for a rescue. He'll ambush anyone who comes along. Even your uncle won't stand a chance against him."

"What do you suggest we do?" Sonya suddenly asked. "He's right outside the door."

Gemma looked around the room then to the ax she held. She indicated the back wall. "Do you know what's on the other side of this wall?"

Sonya shrugged. "The indoor pool, I think," she replied. "You can't possibly be thinking about hacking your way through. He'll hear us and be waiting on the other side."

"I know, but he can't be two places at once," Gemma replied. "You stay by the window and watch for him to leave. When he does, we'll make a run for the fitness room."

"Why hadn't I thought of that?"

Sonya moved to the steam room door and peered out the window. The hammer struck the small window. Sonya ducked and instinctively screamed. Gemma swung the ax for the back wall and splintered the wood with the first blow. Sonya sheepishly looked out the window. The masked killer looked through the window at her. Sonya screamed and moved to the side of the door.

"I really want to go home now," Sonya muttered.

Chapter Thirty-two

*R*avin and Devon walked along the back corridor, each carrying a pool stick for a weapon. Ravin duct taped a filet knife to the thick end of his pool stick as they walked. Devon glanced at him several times and watched him skillfully construct his weapon. His look was serious and determined.

"You know, for a seemingly quiet guy, you can be a little scary," Devon remarked.

"Most sociopaths *are* seemingly quiet."

She stared at him a moment in silence. "Okay, now you're just being creepy," Devon informed him.

Despite the lifted cloud of hallucinations, Ravin was still a mystery to Devon. She sensed his reserve, but he still seemed to be hiding something. Whatever secret he harbored, it almost certainly had to do with the hotel. Most people had secrets, but he kept his hidden even from her highly tuned perception. It felt odd not being able to get much of a read on him.

Devon indicated the doorway toward the end of the corridor. "Let's check the pool area."

"I can't imagine what she'd be doing in there all this time," Ravin announced and cast the roll of duct tape aside. He slashed the air with his newly created weapon.

"Hiding from a psycho killer comes to mind," Devon replied simply.

"That's a dismal thought."

"Just sticking with the theme of your hotel," she informed him. "Helter-Skelter meets Jack the Ripper."

He gave her a stern look. "I have to be honest, Devon, I liked you better when I was flying high on ecstasy."

"Funny; I don't notice any difference in you," she teased while casting a glance at him.

He studied her a moment as they walked. "Do you really see ghosts?"

She rolled her eyes and groaned. "Sure, the one thing you do remember."

"I believe you," he replied and casually looked around as they walked the long, wide corridor.

"You do?"

"Why would you lie?" he asked. "I've seen and felt things within this hotel I can't explain, and it's gotten worse since the mass killings. I always thought the hotel was haunted from the day we broke ground."

"You were here before the hotel was built?" she suddenly asked and appeared curious.

"Since you told me your secret, I suppose I can tell you mine," Ravin replied.

Devon suddenly stopped him in the hallway and turned to look at him. A flood of emotions hit her in a tidal wave. Everything he was hiding suddenly surfaced and all it took was for him to open his mind.

"You own the hotel?"

"How did you know?" he suddenly demanded with a strange look on his face.

"That's what you were about to say, wasn't it?"

"Well, yes," he replied and continued to stare at her. "Is there something else you're not telling me?"

Devon fidgeted but saw no way around hiding her secret any longer. "I'm mildly psychic," she said gently. "I can feel emotions and sometimes read people's thoughts. It's not an exact science, and I can't always translate the vibe someone is sending."

"Sounds like a neat parlor trick," Ravin teased. His look turned serious and his head cocked to the side. "Can you see Gemma? Are you able to find her telepathically or something?"

"I'm afraid it doesn't work that way," Devon replied. "I've heard of others who have amazing abilities, but I don't know that I want that sort of responsibility."

"So maybe you can, but you're unwilling to try," he announced while studying her. His anxiety was escalating. "This is important, Devon. Is Gemma in trouble?"

"I don't do those sorts of parlor tricks, Ravin," she protested. "Nor do I want those abilities."

"So it's not that you can't, but you won't," he growled and turned angry for the first time. Ravin grabbed her arm and stared into her eyes. "Devon, where is Gemma?"

His sudden hostility startled her. It was completely out of character for him, and she didn't need psychic abilities to know that. Devon stared into Ravin's eyes and attempted to empty her mind, but she couldn't stop the flood of emotions pouring into her. She saw Gemma holding her bleeding head while staring at an ax about to strike her. Devon suddenly gasped and clutched her head from the tremendous pain pounding in her skull.

"What did you see?" Ravin demanded with concern.

"It was Gemma," Devon gasped softly. "There was an ax. We need to check the steam room."

Ravin pulled Devon along the hall. She ran after him while clutching her head. Now that the gates had been opened, her mind was flooded with thoughts and images that she didn't want to see. She saw Sonya clutching her bleeding face while screaming. She saw images of Felicia's split skull as blood collected in a pool on the floor. She saw an image of Monica with bloody hands. The more she allowed herself to see, the faster the images came to her. She attempted to keep up with Ravin, but her head was pounding so hard, she thought it would split open.

✝

Sonya slowly peeked out the small window on the steam room door. The ax repeatedly struck the back wall with a series of loud bangs. Gemma had a large portion of the back wall torn away. Sonya looked out the window and became excited.

"I don't see him! He's gone!" Sonya cried out and looked back at Gemma.

Gemma quickly turned toward Sonya and the door. She positioned herself with the ax, stared at the door, and nodded to Sonya. Sonya hesitantly unlocked the door and yanked it open. Gemma stepped into the spa with the ax and looked around. Sonya appeared behind her and looked around as well. Nothing moved. There was no sign of the killer.

"Let's go," Gemma said.

Gemma and Sonya ran across the spa and toward the fitness room door. Both looked at Felicia's battered and bloodied body as they passed. Her head had been split open by the killer's hammer and an enormous amount of blood covered most of the floor surrounding her head. The gruesomeness of the killing sickened both. Gemma and Sonya cautiously entered the fitness room, looked past the exercise machines, and then ran toward the door on the opposite side. Sonya stopped to grab a five-pound dumbbell. They slowed as they approached the door to the main hall. Sonya opened the door and jumped to the side. Gemma stepped into the doorway with her ax prepared to strike. Thankfully, there was no one there. Sonya moved behind Gemma and looked over her shoulder. The main hall was empty. Sonya suddenly hit Gemma on the head with the dumbbell. Gemma gasped and fell to the floor. Sonya tossed the dumbbell aside, picked up the ax, and forcibly rolled Gemma over with her foot. Gemma fell onto her back and didn't move. Sonya sneered at her with a disgusted look.

"Bad news, Gemma," Sonya snarled while spinning the ax in her hands. "Ravin belongs to me."

Sonya raised the ax above her head, prepared to split Gemma's head. Gemma slowly looked up, saw Sonya standing over her with the ax, and rolled out of the path of the crashing blade. The ax struck the marble floor and cracked it. Gemma scrambled to her feet as Sonya raised the ax with an evil, psychotic look.

"Sonya!" Devon was heard yelling from behind her just across the room.

Sonya turned with a startled gasp. Ravin slid across the floor just in front of Sonya and swung the bladed pool stick. The stick struck Sonya across the face and broke. She was thrown backwards and against the wall while dropping the ax. Sonya screamed hysterically, clutched her bleeding face, and ran from the room. Devon checked Gemma for injuries. Ravin quickly straightened, tossed his broken pool stick aside, and pulled Gemma into his arms. She clung to him and sobbed.

"Sonya?" Devon gasped with surprise. "How could it be Sonya?"

"She's insane," Gemma replied while attempting to control her sobs. "She said Ravin belonged to her. She was jealous or something. It doesn't make any sense."

"Let's get you back to our room," Ravin said gently while clinging to her.

"What about Sonya?" Devon asked.

He glared sharply at Devon. "I'll deal with her later," Ravin growled lowly.

As Ravin guided Gemma from the room, Devon grabbed the ax along with her own pool stick and hurried after them.

Chapter Thirty-three

*V*ander and Tyson climbed the ravine by the wrecked cars and looked around for any sign of Novak or Monica. Vander immediately spotted the fresh blood near the back of the Corolla. He hurried to the rear panel of the Corolla and looked at the blood soaking into the ground. Tyson noted the blood, looked alarmed, and visually scanned the area for signs of a dead body or the killer. He looked back at Vander kneeling by the car.

"That's a lot of blood," Tyson said softly. "Someone's in trouble."

Vander straightened and looked around. "Whoever was injured couldn't have gotten far," he announced then looked at the party bus. "We should check the bus."

Vander hurried toward the bus. Tyson skeptically eyed Vander as he walked away and then reluctantly followed. Vander cautiously entered the bus then suddenly stopped to stare at the carefully arranged bodies with a look of shock.

"What sort of whack job are we dealing with?" Vander gasped softly.

Tyson stopped behind Vander, eyed the casually seated corpses, and smirked. "Maybe he just likes his kills neatly arranged."

Vander glared back at Tyson. He wasn't humored by the callus, tasteless remark.

"What?" Tyson scoffed then shook his head. "No sense of humor."

Vander looked away from him with disgust and approached the two bodies out of place lying on the bus floor. He saw the discarded gun sticking out from beneath one of the bodies, appeared alarmed, and picked it up.

"This is Novak's gun," Vander announced with concern and looked around for any other sign of his partner.

Tyson picked up the dart gun and stared at it. He eyed Vander from behind while holding the gun. Vander turned and looked surprised to see the gun in Tyson's hand even though it wasn't aimed at him. Vander's finger tightened on the trigger of Novak's gun still at his side.

"What sort of gun is this?" Tyson asked breaking the tense silence.

Vander relaxed his finger on gun's trigger. "It's a dart gun," he replied while apparently putting the pieces together in his head.

"You mean like a tranquilizer gun?" Tyson asked with a look of surprise.

Vander nodded and stuck Novak's gun down the back of his pants. "That must be how he subdued his victims and was able to kill them at his leisure."

"That explains how he got Darlene on the horse," Tyson remarked then chuckled and shook his head with disgust.

Vander casually removed the dart gun from Tyson, surprising him. Tyson was about to protest then watched as Vander emptied the remaining darts from the gun. He tossed the dart gun aside. It landed with a clatter. He deposited the darts into a glass of water setting alongside one of the dead men.

"What the hell did you do that for?" Tyson demanded and conveyed his disapproval with his expression. "I wouldn't mind having a weapon myself, you know."

"Not that weapon," Vander replied.

Tyson shook his head with disbelief. "You don't trust me, admit it."

Vander casually shrugged. "Okay, I don't trust you."

"That's cold," Tyson muttered.

Vander's silence signaled the discussion was closed for debate. Tyson remained offended then looked around the bus. He indicated the scattered bodies and several overturned objects on the otherwise neatly arranged display.

"Looks like there was a struggle," Tyson informed him.

Vander was frustrated by more than just the disturbing scene as he looked around. "We should see which way that blood leads."

"We're running out of daylight fast," Tyson informed him. "I don't know about you, but I'm not exactly thrilled about being out here after dark."

"My friend could be out there bleeding to death," Vander growled lowly while facing Tyson.

Tyson raised his brows and glared sharply at him. "No offense, but your friend could be hanging from a tree."

Vander stared at him with surprise then sneered and shook his head. "It's difficult to like you."

"I ain't exactly sweet on you either, G-man."

✝

*D*ino stood in the massive kitchen behind the counter and opened a large can of fruit with the industrial sized can opener bolted to the counter. He dumped the contents into a large plastic container, being careful not to spill his dinner. Harris hurried across the kitchen, stopped before Dino, and appeared alarmed.

"I can't find anyone," Harris suddenly announced. "Where the hell did everyone go?"

"What do you mean you can't find anyone?" Dino asked and stared at him. "Did you check the spa? Sonya and Gemma were planning on taking a soak in the hot tub after we'd left."

"I didn't feel like exploring alone," Harris informed him. "I don't like this, Dino. It's too quiet. We should go to the spa and look for Sonya and Gemma."

"Absolutely," he replied while wiping his hands on a dishtowel. "I told them to lock the spa door, but I should make sure Sonya's alright."

Dino suddenly froze and stared past Harris with a look of horror on his face. Sonya stumbled toward them while holding her bleeding cheek. He ran toward her and helped her to the table. She slowly and painfully sat.

"Sonya, what happened?" Dino gasped. His look was somewhere between concern and rage.

She sobbed softly while clinging to her face. "It was Ravin. He attacked me."

"Attacked you?" Dino demanded.

Dino gently pulled Sonya's hand away from her face. Her swollen nose and cheekbone were already black and blue. There was little doubt she had some fractured facial bones. A decent sized gash ran along her cheek and bled freely.

Dino placed the dishtowel to her cut then glared at Harris. "Get her some ice. Keep an eye on her, and don't let her out of your sight."

As Dino started to walk away, Harris stared after him with surprise. "What are you going to do?"

He didn't bother looking back at him. "Kill Ravin," Dino scoffed. "Keep my niece safe or it's your ass, Harris!"

Harris watched Dino storm from the kitchen then looked back at Sonya and became sympathetic. He hurried to the freezer, removed some ice, and returned to her with the bag. He wrapped the ice in a dishtowel and handed it to her.

"What happened to Gemma? She was with you, wasn't she?" Harris asked.

"After Ravin attacked me, she ran away," Sonya said while sniffing and gingerly applied the ice to her bleeding, bruised cheek. "He took off after her. I guess he thought I was dead, so he left me there."

"Did you want me to walk you to your room?" Harris asked timidly. "You can lock yourself in for safekeeping?"

She sniffed, managed a smile, and uncertainly nodded. "I'd like that," she said softly then hesitated. "Although, I could use some painkillers."

"We'll drop by the infirmary on the way to your room," Harris replied. "We should be able to find something in there to help with the pain."

✝

*H*arris rummaged through the drawers in the infirmary while Sonya cleaned the cut on her cheek with antiseptic solution. She looked at her reflection in the mirror and cringed. The left side of her face was swollen nearly twice the size of her right and the dark bruising was only getting worse. The cut wasn't deep but it would definitely leave a scar. She looked at the dishtowel on the counter before her, set her bloodied cloth aside, and carefully opened the

170

dishtowel to reveal a dart gun. Harris turned with a bottle of pills in his hand.

"Found some heavy-duty painkillers," he announced and seemed pleased with himself.

Sonya turned to face him and aimed the dart gun at him. He stared at the strange gun with surprise and possible horror.

"What the hell--?" As he stared at the gun, he let out a relieved sigh and shook his head. "You scared me for a minute there. Where did you find that? What is that? A BB gun?"

"This?" she asked while grinning. "No, this is a tranquilizer gun. The darts knock you out in minutes--sometimes seconds."

Harris stared at her and his concern quickly returned. "What are you doing with it?"

"I'm going to shoot you with it, Harris," she casually replied while smiling sweetly. "It'll be lights out, so you won't squirm when I cut you open."

"You're joking, right?" he suddenly gasped. "There's no way you're behind this. You wouldn't kill people. That's not who you are."

She laughed lowly. "Who do you think poisoned all those people in the dining room? I'll admit I had a little help slitting the wrists of all those people in the pool area before joining the others in the lounge. A can of knockout mist only lasts so long. You can't dillydally or they'll wake up before you've finished." She playfully frowned. "And we didn't want anyone feeling any pain. That would be cruel."

The look on Harris' face conveyed his fears. "Sonya, please," he said gently. "We had a moment together. You don't want to kill me. I could make it worth your while. I have money."

"It's not just about money, Harris," she said while groaning then raised her brows. "And our moment? Please!" Her smile mocked him. "That was just a two-minute distraction for appearances. I have my sights a little higher."

Sonya squeezed the trigger. Harris dove from the dart's path, narrowly avoiding the little dart. The dart hit the glass on the medicine cupboard and pierced it. Sonya aimed again. Harris shoved the rolling cart across the room and struck her in the legs, throwing her momentarily off balance. He ran from the infirmary and along the corridor with Sonya several yards behind him. As he approached the lobby, the elevator door stood open. He bolted into the elevator and hit the close button several times. Sonya appeared as the doors closed, shutting her out. Harris leaned against the elevator wall while breathing heavily. He snorted a soft laugh of relief then looked at his arm. A little dart was embedded in his lower arm.

Harris groaned softly. "That's just perfect."

Chapter Thirty-four

Several candles flickered and burned around the exam room in the vet's office, brightening the small room. Novak sat on the exam table with his shirt and pants off while Monica stitched his arm. The cut on his thigh was already stitched with what appeared to be 'M' stitches. Novak grinned while appearing overly sedated, obviously feeling no pain while Monica stitched his cuts. He pointed at the 'M' stitches on his thigh and laughed.

"M for Monica," he teased.

"You got that all on your own? Good for you," she announced with a smirk across her face. She seemed more alert now than she had less than an hour ago. The effects of the dart were obviously wearing off.

"I've been branded," he chuckled then held his head. "That's some pretty serious shit you injected me with. What was in that syringe?"

"Local sedation--for dogs," she replied. "And apparently, I gave you too much."

"No, it's good stuff. I'm so lucky to have such a smart, sexy, and *lethal* girlfriend."

She cast a glare at him. "Who the hell said I was your girlfriend?"

He gave her an innocent look and seemed offended by the question. "The guy who tried to kill me."

Monica rolled her eyes then finished stitching him. She dressed his wounds with fresh gauze then washed his blood from her hands. Novak's look turned serious despite his sedated state.

"You know, I was drugged last night," he announced boldly. "If I performed poorly--"

Monica dried her hands then casually tossed him his pants, startling him. Novak caught his pants and eyed her.

"There was nothing wrong with your performance," she informed him with little interest.

Novak made an effort to slip into his pants from where he sat on the exam table. He kept missing the pants leg with his foot despite several attempts.

"So then what's the problem?" he asked.

Novak finally got his feet into the pants, attempted to pull them up, and fell to the floor with a thud. Monica casually looked at him as he lie on the floor, face down.

"Ouch--"

Monica groaned and helped him to his feet. He finished pulling his pants up and looked at her.

"I never said there was a problem," she remarked without looking at him.

"Certainly seemed like there was."

Monica glared at him and cleverly raised her brows. "I'd spent the last eight years running with the big boys in the military. If I wanted to be taken seriously, I needed to prove I was one of them," she remarked. "There's little room for emotion when the man you'd just screwed is blown apart the next day."

He stared at her and was surprised. "The man you loved was killed?"

"I didn't love him," she retorted tersely. "I was just screwing him."

Novak stiffly slipped into his shirt and glanced at Monica, who now avoided looking at him. Her stern look turned serious and possibly angry.

"He died because of me," she announced hotly. "If he hadn't been following me around like some lovesick schoolboy, he wouldn't be dead!"

"The way I followed you--?"

She suddenly turned to face him and stared into his eyes. "I didn't need your help! I didn't ask for your help! You nearly got yourself killed. And for what?" she suddenly demanded. "Because we slept together?"

"Going after bad guys and protecting people is kind of what I do, in case you'd forgotten," he lashed back at her. "And maybe you need to be reminded from time to time that you're not a one-woman commando unit either." His anger seemed to boil over. "If you trusted me to cover your ass, maybe I wouldn't have needed to follow you in the first place."

Monica glared at Novak with a look of annoyance. He stared back at her without flinching. Monica suddenly grabbed him by the face and kissed him passionately. Novak was momentarily startled but quickly returned the kiss. Without warning, she threw him down on the exam table and jumped on top of him.

✝

Vander and Tyson entered the lobby from the outside entrance while bickering at one another. The argument had apparently been going on for quite some time, and neither man was too pleased with the other. Sonya leaned against the wall next to the elevator with a bloodied rag in her hand. She stared at them with a look of fright. Tyson immediately saw her battered face and ran toward her. She clutched the bloodstained rag as he approached. He gently touched her face and looked at her injuries.

"What happened?" Tyson suddenly demanded as his rage increased. "Who did this to you?"

"It was Ravin," Sonya gasped softly. "Uncle Dino went after him. I don't know what came over Ravin, but he beat Felicia to death with a hammer in the spa." She sobbed softly. "When I tried to stop him, he attacked me."

"I knew it!" Tyson cried out. "I knew that bastard was the killer!"

Tyson violently struck the elevator button. When the elevator didn't immediately arrive, he grabbed Novak's gun from the back of Vander's pants, and took off down the hallway toward the stairs.

"Tyson," Vander called after him with surprise. "Come back here!"

Vander shook his head with disgust then looked at the severely battered Sonya. He stared at her injuries and was almost horrified by her appearance. Vander attempted a soothing tone to comfort the obviously hurting young woman.

"I need to stop Tyson before he does something stupid," Vander remarked. "On my way, I'll take you someplace safe."

"Yeah?" she scoffed then laughed softly. "Where's someplace safe?"

"You can hole up in my guestroom while I go after Tyson," he gently informed her. Vander pressed the elevator button and again looked at her injuries. He was curious. "Are you sure it was a hammer?" he asked while studying her. "Your injuries don't look like they were caused by a hammer. Looks more like a policeman's nightstick."

The elevator doors opened to reveal Harris lying dead in a pool of blood. Vander saw the mangled body on the elevator floor, quickly entered the elevator, and crouched alongside Harris's body. He'd been stabbed multiple times before having his throat slashed. The kill wasn't nearly as neat with him as with the others. This kill was a little more personal in nature. Vander shook his head while staring at Harris' body. Sonya allowed the bloodied rag to fall to the floor to reveal the dart gun in her hand. She raised the dart gun and casually shot Vander, hitting him in the shoulder. He jumped with surprise, looked at the dart gun, and attempted to stand. He clutched his head and immediately collapsed to the floor alongside Harris' blood-soaked body.

Sonya removed the semiautomatic from Vander's shoulder holster, straightened, and aimed it at him while grinning deviously. "Good-bye, Agent Hawk."

As she was about to pull the trigger, her wrist was suddenly grabbed and the gun violently snatched from her. She turned to face the badly beaten and bloody Cody.

"Daddy," Sonya gasped with surprise and stared at his bleeding and broken face. "What happened?"

"Ran into a little trouble with that bitch, Monica, and that prick, Novak," Cody snarled. He then indicated Vander. "I want this one alive. I need him as bait for his partner. Novak will kill himself trying to save him."

"But I want to kill him," Sonya whined.

"In good time," he replied then indicated Vander's unconscious body. "Help me move him someplace a little more private. We wouldn't want anyone finding him before we're ready."

Sonya helped her father move Vander's unconscious body from the elevator.

"I saw Tyson running up the stairs," Cody remarked. "Where was that brother of yours going on fire like that?"

"To kill Ravin," she replied and immediately appeared concerned. "You won't let him, will you? You know I want Ravin for myself."

Cody rolled his eyes and shook his head. "I don't know what you see in that one."

Chapter Thirty-five

$\mathcal{D}$evon stood before the large windows within Ravin's corner suite and looked out across the darkened resort grounds. Her head still pounded, but she was able to stop the images from flashing through her mind for the time being. There was little point to having a gift if it couldn't be controlled. She felt as if she was free-falling and no one could catch her. She was confused by everything she was feeling. Did she actually help save Gemma? If she opened her mind, would she be able to stop others from dying? Would she be able to see the killer for who he really was? It was almost too much for her to comprehend. And if she did open her mind, what if she couldn't control it? After the first few seconds, the images no longer made sense. It was just an endless loop of horror scenes and violence. How would turning herself into a basket case help anyone? Ravin walked out of the bedroom, shut the door, and then approached the minibar. He opened a bottle of wine in silence and poured each of them a glass. Devon studied Ravin and gently rubbed her chilled arms.

"How is she?" she asked.

Ravin approached Devon with both glasses of wine and extended one to her. She accepted the glass while watching him.

"She's holding up pretty well considering she was nearly chopped apart with an ax," Ravin muttered and sipped his wine. He was obviously preoccupied and most definitely hostile.

"It's my fault, isn't it?" she asked softly. "If I would have acted sooner--"

Ravin stared at her with surprise and shook his head. "No, Devon, you did a great job. You saved Gemma." He took a deep breath and looked out the window into the darkness. "I'm the one who should be apologizing to you. I made you do something you clearly didn't want to do, and I'm going to guess you've been avoiding doing that for a long time."

"I can't control it," she said softly while staring at her glass of wine. "I'm not strong enough."

He turned to face her. "That's bullshit," Ravin remarked sternly. "You just haven't developed it yet. You can control it, and you're most certainly strong enough."

She didn't want to have this conversation. "I should see if Vander is back and warn him about Sonya," she announced while setting her glass of wine down on a nearby end table.

"No," he growled, alarming her with his gruff tone. "I don't want you going anywhere alone. You're my responsibility. Vander knows you're with me. When he returns, he'll know to look for you here."

She stared at him and wasn't sure how to react to his hostile mood. "Okay, you're acting a little creepy, Ravin," Devon announced. "What's wrong?"

"What's wrong?" he scoffed. "My girlfriend was nearly butchered by a disturbed, sociopathic bitch wielding an ax, and you want to go traipsing around the hotel by yourself." His look was frightening to her. "Whether you're seeking permission or not, the answer is no."

Devon stared at him with surprise and concern. She slowly sat on the arm of a nearby chair and studied him. She knew something more was bothering him. Perhaps it was a feeling of helplessness. Or did he feel guilty about not killing Sonya with the first swing? She was afraid to open her mind even a little to dig deeper for an answer. She was afraid of what would happen, what her mind would show her.

Ravin groaned softly, allowing his shoulders to sag, and avoided looking at her. "I've never lost control like that before," he said softly as if answering her silent question. "I'd never even thought about striking a woman in my life, but I wanted to kill Sonya."

"But you didn't kill her."

He suddenly glared at her. "That's because my pool stick broke and she took off. Believe me, Devon, given the opportunity; I would have taken her head off without thinking twice."

She stared at him and wondered if she should be concerned. He was definitely on the edge of sanity. Not only did she have Ravin to contend with, but also her concern for Vander was getting the better of her. If she just opened her mind, would she be able to see if he was okay? What if something happened to him? She wasn't sure she could handle seeing his death playing out like some homemade horror movie. There was an urgent pounding on the door, alarming both. Devon jumped to her feet and looked at the bolted door. Ravin snatched her pool stick from the coffee table and approached the door. Devon grabbed the ax and joined him. Ravin looked through the peek hole.

"Ravin!" Tyson yelled from outside the door. "I know you're in there, you son-of-a-bitch! Open this fucking door or I'll break it down!"

"Ravin's not here," Devon suddenly yelled back. "Considering your sister tried to kill Gemma, there's no way I'm letting you in either!"

"What the fuck are you talking about?" Tyson demanded. "Ravin tried to kill Sonya! He busted her face open right after he killed Felicia!"

"If Ravin hadn't struck Sonya with that pool stick, Gemma would be dead," Devon yelled back.

"Pool stick?" Tyson suddenly demanded. "She said he struck her with a hammer!"

"A hammer?" Devon scoffed while staring at the door beyond Ravin. She suddenly laughed. "Think about it, Tyson. If Ravin had hit her in the face with a hammer, she'd have a hole in her skull!"

There was silence from the closed door. Ravin and Devon exchanged looks. The sound of running feet could be heard in the hallway leading away from the door. Ravin looked out the peek hole then back at Devon.

"He's heading for the stairs," Ravin announced.

"Do you think he's warning her?"

"I don't know, but I think things are about to get ugly fast," Ravin informed her. "I need to find Agent Hawk, assuming he made it back with Tyson, and warn him."

"What about Gemma?"

"You stay with Gemma and don't open this door," he ordered sternly.

"I'm going with you, Ravin," Devon said. "You need someone to watch your back."

"We'll both watch your back," Gemma announced from across the room.

Ravin and Devon looked toward the bedroom. Gemma stood in the doorway clutching a fire poker.

"I'm taking that bitch down," Gemma scoffed with a hateful scowl on her face.

Ravin stared at Gemma and opened his mouth to protest. He sank into thought then closed his mouth and groaned softly. "Fine," he reluctantly replied. "But if we're going out there together, we need to be prepared."

Devon indicated the ax in her hand and silently responded with her eyes. Gemma slapped the fire poker against her palm, indicating she was prepared as well. There was an awkward silence. Ravin stared at Devon.

"Where's Sonya?" he asked firmly.

Gemma glanced from Ravin to Devon with a look of bewilderment. Devon considered protesting and claiming diminished psychic capacity, but the look on Ravin's face said he wasn't going to accept that response. His stare left no room for protest. Devon took a deep breath and opened her mind just enough to allow a few images inside. The images flooded into her mind in a sudden rush. She clutched her head and attempted to close her mind. She saw Vander lying on the floor in the dining room among the dead bodies. There was a bloody baseball bat and a woman's scream. Devon gasped. Vander was in trouble! Devon clung to her head and looked at Ravin.

"The dining room," she gasped softly while attempting to control her heavy breathing. "We should check the dining room."

Ravin studied her a moment then nodded. "Okay, we'll check the dining room," he said gently then gave her a reassuring look. "You're doing fine, Devon. We need you. Don't fight it. What you see could be the difference between life and death for us."

"You're putting too much faith into my abilities, Ravin," she announced and slowly lowered her hand from her head. "I see images, nothing more. It's impossible to know what they even mean, if anything."

"You were right about Gemma and the ax," Ravin insisted. "If you're in doubt, tell me what you see, and I'll translate it for you. I'll take responsibility if my interpretation is wrong."

Devon looked at the ax in her hand. She suddenly saw an image of the ax penetrating someone's body with blood erupting from the wound. She gasped softly and dropped the ax with a clatter. Gemma and Ravin looked at her with surprise.

"What did you see?" he asked while picking up the ax.

Devon stared at the ax in his hand. "Someone is killed with the ax," she gasped softly.

"Who?" Gemma cried out softly.

"I don't know," she said with a shaken breath and subconsciously rubbed her own abdomen.

Ravin watched her then looked at the ax he held. He looked back at Devon. "Was it you?"

She trembled slightly, drew a shaken breath, and shook her head. "I--I don't know."

"Do you want to wait here?" Ravin asked.

She drew a deep breath, straightened proudly, and took the ax from him. "No, I have to go," Devon replied.

"No, you don't have to go," he insisted. "Maybe the two of you should stay here."

Devon stared back at Ravin. "I have to go," she insisted. "*They* want me there."

"They?" Gemma asked with surprise.

"The ghosts?" Ravin questioned.

"I think so," Devon replied. "We need to go."

Chapter Thirty-six

$\mathcal{V}$ander slowly woke within the gym to Sonya hovering over him with a devious, twisted smile on her battered and bruised face. He gasped and immediately fought against the ropes binding him to an exercise machine. He was tied in such a fashion as if he'd been working out. His ankles were tied beneath the padded bar on the leg extension while he straddled the bench, and his wrists were tied to the pec deck handles on either side of his head. Sonya seductively flaunted a large hunting knife while keeping her body close to his.

"I'm not allowed to kill you just yet," Sonya informed him. "We're waiting for some of your friends, and then we're going to have a little party."

Sonya seductively ran the knife along Vander's chest then mounted him, straddling his hips in a sexually compromising position while half sitting on his lap. She placed her arms around his neck and gently ran the blade of the knife along the back of his neck. Her face was only inches from his as she smiled lustfully and brushed her lips past his. Vander showed no reaction while staring at her.

"It's going to be wild fun," she cooed softly.

"Untie me, and I'll show you how much fun I can be," he announced while raising a devious brow.

"Hmm, I like your enthusiasm," Sonya said sweetly, "but I'm saving that for Ravin." She moved off his lap and casually walked away from him.

"Didn't he break your face?"

Sonya frowned and gingerly touched her swollen, bruised, and bandaged cheek. She looked back at Vander and again smiled lustfully. "I'm willing to forgive him," she replied.

"You know, nothing against the creepy, little guy, but what's your interest in him?" he asked.

"He's filthy rich," she replied. "Despite what he tells people, he owns this hotel, the one hundred acres surrounding it, and most of the town." She grinned and seemed pleased with herself. "I've got a special 'love drug' just for him. That whore Gemma is going to watch while he violates me three ways to Sunday. And right after we're finished, I'm going to gut her." Her pleased grin was disturbing. "Then Ravin will be all mine along with this hotel and the town."

"Do you honestly think your accomplice will allow him to live?"

"As long as he remains drugged, I'm allowed to keep him," she insisted while maintaining her grin.

"Sounds like someone is lying to you," Vander announced simply and appeared disinterested. "I've seen it many times before. The young, gullible accomplice falls for it every time."

Her look turned hostile or possibly concerned that he might be telling the truth. "You're wrong."

"You're being set up," Vander announced while chuckling softly in his throat. "He's trying to appease you long enough to frame you for the killings. You'll take the fall, and he'll reap the rewards and get off free and clear."

"Daddy!"

Cody hurried from the men's locker room while clutching his wrapped ribs and limped toward her with an irritated look. "Damn it, Sonya. What's wrong with you?" he demanded. "You're supposed to keep it quiet. What if someone comes here before we're ready?"

"He's pissing me off," she pouted with the appearance of a little girl. "Can I kill him?"

"No, not until I say so," Cody replied firmly. "You know we need him."

"He says you're going to double-cross me," she whined. "Make him shut up."

Cody groaned softly, gently took Sonya's face in his hands, and stared into her eyes. "Don't listen to him. He's trying to work on your psyche--what little you have," he informed her. "You're my daughter, and I love you. I would never do anything to hurt you, would I?"

She frowned. "No, of course not."

"That's my baby."

Cody leaned closer and kissed Sonya passionately on the mouth. Vander stared in astonishment as Sonya returned the kiss with all the exoticness of a lover. Cody broke off the kiss, smiled, and took the knife from her.

"I'll handle this," Cody informed her. "You go find that brother of yours, before he does something stupid."

Sonya smiled and left the fitness room through the spa doorway. Cody limped painfully toward Vander while studying him. Vander watched him and attempted to hide his disgust at what he had just witnessed.

"You two are rather *close*," Vander muttered.

"You've got a big mouth," Cody growled lowly. "I think you need something else to think about, so you'll stop harassing my daughter--like wondering how far your left testicle will roll across the floor."

Vander looked emotionless but his entire body tensed in response to the threat. Cody held up the knife, chuckled softly, and grabbed Vander's pants. Vander gasped and his expression immediately dropped from Cody's sudden movement.

Cody grinned deviously. "This may hurt a little--"

A gun was heard cocking just a few feet away. Cody tensed while slowly straightening but kept the knife close to Vander's face. He cast a glance alongside him. Tyson stood only a few feet away with Novak's gun aimed at his father.

"This isn't how it looks," Cody explained and managed a humored smile.

"Looks like you plan to castrate the man," Tyson growled under his breath.

"Oh, then it is how it looks," his father muttered without removing the knife from Vander's face.

"Drop the knife."

"Everything I did, I did for you and Sonya," Cody informed him and still didn't move.

"Oh really? How long have you been fucking your own daughter?" Tyson's rage exploded to the surface. His finger tightened on the trigger. "Drop the knife, or so help me, I'll blow your brains out," he snarled with conviction.

"You want our town back, don't you?" Cody demanded while casting a sideways glance at his son.

"You have until three, you sick fuck," Tyson growled while sneering at his father.

"They had to die," Cody explained while raising his brows and clutching the knife. "The hotel needed to fail."

"One--"

"All those tourists were ruining our town--our woods," Cody protested to his son while staring at Vander. "You said so yourself, remember?"

"Two--"

"Damn it! I'm your father!" Cody yelled at Tyson while turning his head to look at him. "You do what I say!"

Tyson pulled the trigger without flinching. His father's head snapped back to a dead center head shot as blood and brains erupted out the back of his skull. He collapsed to the floor.

Tyson's look remained emotionless. "Three."

Vander stared with surprise at Cody's lifeless body as blood rapidly spilled from his head. He hesitantly looked at Tyson, who slowly lowered the gun. The door from the spa was thrown open to reveal Sonya. She saw her father lying on the floor in a pool of rapidly collecting blood near Vander's feet.

"Daddy!"

Tyson suddenly aimed the gun at Sonya. She saw him, gasped, and darted back into the spa. The gun fired twice. Sonya stepped back into the doorway with Vander's gun and fired at Tyson. Tyson took a shot to his arm. He leaped to the floor and immediately fired back at Sonya. Her gun clicked empty. She gasped as Tyson aimed and fired. She disappeared into the spa. The bullet struck the doorframe. Tyson straightened and again pulled the trigger. His gun clicked empty. He cast the gun aside with disgust and looked at his bleeding arm.

"Son-of-a-bitch!"

Tyson grabbed the discarded knife and quickly approached Vander. Vander tensed at the sight of the knife in Tyson's hand.

He glared at Vander and appeared offended. "I just saved your ass, and you still don't trust me?" Tyson demanded. He shook his head and cut the ropes to Vander's wrists and ankles. "You have some major trust issues, G-man."

Vander jumped to his feet. "We have to stop her," he blurted out. "She wants Gemma dead."

"So I heard. Gemma's safe with Devon in Ravin's suite," Tyson informed him. "Besides, it's not Sonya you need to worry about. My father could never have orchestrated something this big. My uncle's behind this, and he's not going to go down so easily."

"Okay, so this is Dino's party," Vander announced. "Where will we find him?"

"Looking for Ravin," Tyson replied. "He hurt Sonya. He'll want to make him suffer."

"We need to go to Ravin's suite."

"Devon said he wasn't there."

"She lied," Vander informed him. "He wouldn't leave Devon and Gemma alone, and if he tried, Devon would follow him. Trust me; he's there."

Chapter Thirty-seven

Ravin cautiously entered the dining room with Devon and Gemma following closely behind him. All three made faces from the foul stench of decaying bodies that lingered within the massive room. They scanned the large room filled with dead bodies seated and posed around the tables. Devon watched the ghosts circulating around the room as if looking for something or perhaps just some answers. They wouldn't know peace until their bodies were laid to rest. At least that was how it usually worked in Devon's experience. She'd never been a witness to such violent, mass death before, so she was still attempting to make sense of their behavior. Ravin stopped both women with a raised hand and scanned the room with a sweeping look. He hesitated and, with a nod, indicated a woman with strawberry blonde hair seated at the table with her back to them. From behind, the woman could have been Sonya.

Hiding among the battlefield of dead corpses was genius. It seemed almost improbable that Sonya would think of something that clever. They silently approached the blonde woman from behind. Ravin poked her in the shoulder with his pool stick. The dead, decayed woman collapsed across the table, startling all three. Gemma groaned softly and held her chest. Sonya suddenly leaped up behind Gemma from a nearby table and hit her over the head with an empty, glass water pitcher. As the glass pitcher shattered against her head, Gemma gasped and fell to the floor. Sonya grabbed Gemma's discarded fire poker as Ravin swung at her with the pool stick. She blocked the pool stick with the fire poker and grinned.

"Not this time," Sonya scoffed.

Sonya kicked Ravin in the groin. He dropped to his knees while clutching himself in agony. Devon lunged for Sonya with the ax. Sonya gasped with surprise as the ax was swung for her chest. The ax handle was suddenly grabbed, abruptly stopping Devon's assault. She came face-to-face with Dino, who forcibly slung her around, easily pulling the ax from her hands. Devon flew across the floor and slid a couple of feet from Dino's powerful thrust. Sonya stood over Devon and swung the fire poker at her head. Devon gasped with alarm and swept Sonya's feet out from under her. Sonya fell roughly onto her backside. Dino clutched the ax and lunged for Ravin, who still remained on his knees. Vander suddenly tackled Dino to the floor. The ax flew from his hands and slid beneath one of the tables. As they rolled, Dino landed on top of Vander and punched him in the face. Tyson was suddenly standing over them and kicked Dino in the side, knocking him off Vander. Vander immediately jumped to his feet at the same time as Dino. Ravin slowly crawled across the floor toward the table with the ax handle partially exposed beneath it. Devon lunged for the discarded fire poker. Just as she reached the poker, Sonya kicked her in the ribs. Devon fell to the floor and gasped with surprise and agony. Sonya pulled her to her feet by her hair and held a hunting knife to her throat from behind.

"Stop! Anyone moves, and I slice her!"

All eyes were suddenly on Sonya with the knife to Devon's throat. Dino smirked and kicked Vander in the groin. As Vander clutched himself and doubled over, Dino punched him in the head, driving him the rest of the way to the floor. Ravin remained on his hands and knees with one hand on the ax handle. Sonya glared at Ravin while pressing the knife against Devon's throat.

"Move away from that ax," Sonya growled.

Ravin slowly moved to his knees. The ax was just within his reach. He stared at Sonya holding Devon from behind and appeared to await an opportunity. The ghosts circled Devon and stared at her with frightened looks. As she stared back, she realized they feared for her life. Devon's expression dropped as she stared back at the ghosts. She feared she'd soon be joining them, but something was telling her to listen to them. There were too many to make out any one face as they continued to move closer to her, surrounding her. They were determined to talk to her. She knew her life and the lives of her friends depended on her opening her mind to them. She needed to let them in. Devon relaxed her mind. The spirits came at her like a tidal wave. Every emotion, every moment, and every thought they'd had invaded her mind. The pressure in her head was overwhelming!

Dino took two steps toward Tyson and glared into his eyes with a hateful, demanding look. "You'd go against your own family for these people?"

"I was doing just fine with *these people*," Tyson snarled at his uncle. "What did my family ever do for me? My family can all go to hell!"

Dino struck Tyson in the throat. Tyson gasped, wheezed, and fell to his knees while clutching his throat.

He sneered at his nephew and calmly pointed a warning finger at him. "I'll deal with you later, boy," Dino snarled then approached Ravin, who remained on his knees with an emotionless expression. Dino grinned psychotically. "I'll give you credit, Ravin. I never expected a rich, little fuck like you to hold up this well under these conditions. You have to know what's coming--" Dino casually removed the ax from beneath the table and straightened with a smile. "--yet you don't show any fear." He was humored. "I admire that, and I want to break you at the same time." Dino casually looked around the room and wore a cheerful smile on his psychotic face. "I know, let's play a game." He flipped the ax skillfully in his hand. "We'll call it 'jigsaw puzzle'." He grinned deviously at Ravin. "But don't worry; you'll be the last contestant. I want you to see what happens to the others before you share their fate. I want to see the look of fear on your face."

Ravin slowly moved to his feet and stared into Dino's eyes with little emotion. "I don't fear death, Dino. Do you?"

"You can't intimidate me," he replied with a humored chuckle.

"It's not intimidation, it's extermination," Ravin replied calmly. "This hotel is tainted with blood. The only logical conclusion is to destroy it and start over. That's why I started a fire in the basement."

"Bullshit."

"When the fire alarm sounds, that means the fire has reached the furnace room, where gas is quickly filling," Ravin casually informed him. "Once it reaches the furnace room--" He mouthed the word 'boom'.

Sonya seemed alarmed and looked from Ravin to her uncle while clutching the knife against Devon's throat. Dino stared at Ravin's serious look. There was no indication in his eyes that he was bluffing.

"Uncle Dino--?" Sonya gasped.

Her uncle glared at her and appeared irritated by her paranoia. "He'd never blow up the hotel, Sonya," Dino snapped. "Don't be so gullible."

The fire alarm suddenly wailed, breaking the silence, causing everyone to jump. Dino and Sonya looked around with surprise to the blaring fire alarm.

Ravin slowly shook his head and smirked deviously. "Whether you want to believe it or not, I'm more of a monster than you could ever be."

Devon stared at the collection of ghosts standing before her, staring at her. She could almost make out their faces now. There were more than before. They were all collecting in the dining room, surrounding her. Once she opened her mind to them, they were drawn to her from every corner. She saw every horrifying detail of their deaths. Their hollowed out bodies, their slit throats, their slashed wrists, and bloated bodies. She could feel their pain. She could hear them talking. They whispered to her, speaking directly at her. Just the fact that the spirits were talking to her was alarming enough, but they kept coming. More and more spirits collected around her until they were all present, even those from the bus. As several stood in front of her and whispered to her, the remaining ghosts whirled around her and Sonya, creating a gust of wind. The ghosts were no longer frightened; they were angry. As the unprovoked wind blew past Sonya, she gasped and looked around with fear in her eyes.

Devon stared at the ghosts standing before her and attempted to listen to their words. Her head no longer pounded, and the images of horror began to collect and play out in sequence like some frightening movie. She could see what happened to them as it unfolded. She saw every gruesome detail as if she had been there. She saw the razor dragging across their wrists while feeling pain of the blade as if it was happening to her. She saw Cody gutting the bodies as they hung from the trees, all while feeling the sting of the knife being dragged through her own midsection. She heard the metallic clatter as the can of knockout mist rolled along the aisle of the bus and watched as the crash survivors gasped and passed out. She saw Cody systematically kill them one by one. The ghosts in front of her continued to speak, pulling her from the horror movie playing in her head. They were nearly impossible to understand, almost as if they spoke a foreign language. She desperately wanted to hear them. Ghosts had never spoken to her before, and she needed to know what they wanted from her. She had to open her mind further and let them in. Devon was no longer aware of her current surroundings. All that mattered were the ghosts standing before her and the words they were muttering.

"I don't understand?" she said softly in response. "What are you saying?"

Sonya was frightened while keeping the knife to Devon's throat and nervously looked around as the wind blew past them in a whirlwind. "Who are you talking to? What's going on?" she cried out with fear.

Devon continued her conversation with the ghosts and was no longer aware of Sonya's mindless chatter. The ghostly voices grew louder and became clearer. She was finally able to hear them.

"It was her?" Devon suddenly asked with surprise. "She poisoned the others? How do you know that?"

Sonya was now stricken with panic. "Who are you talking to? Shut up! Shut up!" She looked at her uncle, who also stared at the paranormal activity within the dining room. "Uncle Dino, make her shut up!"

"When did she tell you that?" Devon asked.

The whispering continued and became louder. It wasn't clear whether or not Sonya heard the whispered voices. Sonya continued to look around as the spirits begin to circle them in a small tornado. Both women's hair blow above them. Dino now became alarmed as well and clutched the ax. Despite the bizarre events surrounding Devon and Sonya, Ravin didn't take his eyes off Dino.

"She's doing something!" Sonya screamed.

"Damn it, just kill her," Dino shouted.

Sonya attempted to slit Devon's throat, but the ghosts surrounding her grabbed her wrist and kept her from killing Devon. Devon was unaware of it. Sonya screamed and attempted to pull away from the ghostly hands clutching her wrist. The ghostly hands were all over her. Dino suddenly sneered, raised the ax, and lunged for Devon, prepared to strike. Ravin grabbed a fork from the table and rammed it into Dino's neck. Dino cried out with surprise and agony. He struck Ravin in the chest with the ax handle. Ravin clutched his chest from the blunt force and immediately dropped to his knees. Dino pulled the bloody fork from his neck and was further enraged by what he considered to be a nuisance wound.

"That was right before she killed you?" Devon asked the ghost standing directly in front of her. "Is that why you're here? Is that why you want to help me?"

"Who are you talking to?" Sonya shouted in fear while fighting the ghostly hands holding her wrist.

Sonya desperately wanted to kill Devon but the spirits prevented it. She struggled to hold onto Devon, who made no attempt to pull free from her grip. Devon slowly turned to face Sonya as the knife was held back by the ghosts. She looked into Sonya's eyes with a chilling expression.

"Harris is pissed--"

Sonya appeared horrified by her words. Dino cried out and swung the ax at Devon. Harris's ghost shoved Devon to the floor and out of the path of the swinging blade. The ax went straight through Harris' ghostly body and impaled Sonya in the abdomen. Sonya suddenly gasped, spit up blood, and stared with horror into her uncle's eyes. Dino stared back with the realization of what he'd done.

"Harris--?" Sonya gasped while seemingly staring through her uncle.

Devon flipped onto her backside on the floor and looked up. Dino stared with horror at the ax embedded in Sonya's blood-soaked midsection. He pulled the ax free and watched as her body lifelessly collapsed to the floor. Sonya's spirit remained standing and stared into Harris's ghostly eyes.

Harris smiled evilly. "Now it's my turn."

Sonya's spirit screamed. Both spirits erupted into light and zipped from the room. Dino stared at Sonya's blood-soaked body on the floor near Devon. He glared at Devon, cried out, and raised the ax above his head. Devon gasped with horror. A loud female scream was heard, sending alarm through the others. As the ax came down, a swinging baseball bat collided with it. The ax flew from Dino's hands and slid across the room. Dino turned with surprise and stared at Monica. She clung to her bloodstained baseball bat and glared at Dino with a psychotic look on her stern face.

"That's my friend," Monica growled lowly. "You want a piece of her? You have to go through me."

Monica casually tossed the bat aside and stood directly in front of Dino.

Dino eyed Monica, seemed stunned, and then sneered with annoyance. "You're the bitch who broke my brother's face," he growled.

"Oh, the pussy survived?" Monica scoffed then snorted a laugh. "What do you know?"

"I'm going to tear the flesh from your body one piece at a time," Dino snarled.

"Bring it on, old man," Monica said lowly. "I hope you're more of a challenge than that 40% proof brother of yours."

Novak limped into the dining room, approached Vander, and painfully knelt alongside him where he remained on the floor. Vander looked at his partner, appeared alarmed, and struggled to pull himself to his feet.

"Do something." Vander gasped while clutching his head. "He's going to kill her!"

Novak grinned. "My money's on my girl."

Tyson slowly crawled toward them while barely able to breath and indicated the nearby fire poker. "The poker," he pleaded in a raspy voice. "Take him out."

Monica took a boxing stance and stared directly into Dino's eyes. Dino squared off and swung at her. Monica dodged his fist and spun into a roundhouse kick, nailing Dino in the ribs. Dino attempted to kick back at her, but she was already in a return kick the opposite direction and nailed him in the chest. Dino stumbled backwards, looked irritated, and lunged for her. Monica dodged his fist and punched back, striking him in the nose. He jumped back with surprise and touched his bleeding nose.

"Are you fighting or initiating foreplay?" Monica remarked while sneering at him.

Dino slung the blood from his hand and swung for Monica. Monica flew into a series of kicks, punches, and flips, bending Dino around her like a rag doll. She flipped him over her and caught him around the neck while dropping him to his knees. Dino gasped and struggled against her arm locked around his neck from behind. Monica looked down at him with little emotion and almost no exertion.

"This is the part where I snap your neck," Monica casually informed him.

The room was eerily silent as everyone stared at them with anticipation. Monica released Dino and punched him forcibly in the face. He fell to the floor with a gasp and was unable to move. Monica sneered at him and straightened proudly.

"But I don't kill pussies."

Monica walked away from him and approached Novak, who smiled and painfully straightened.

"You were awesome," Novak announced.

Monica grabbed him by the face and kissed him passionately. He immediately returned the kiss. Ravin hurried to Gemma's fallen side and pulled her into his arms. She slowly woke, appeared concerned, and looked at him. He smiled and held her. Devon snapped out of her trance and hurried to Vander's fallen side. As she kneeled alongside him, he clung to her with a relieved sigh. He looked up at Ravin with concern.

"What about the fire in the basement?" Vander asked.

"There's no fire," Novak answered for Ravin. "Ravin saw me in the doorway and signaled me. When he said he'd set a fire, I pulled the fire alarm."

"I was just trying to buy some time," Ravin informed them then glared at Novak. "What the hell took you so long to intervene?"

"Sonya had a knife to Devon's throat," Novak protested. "What did you want me to do?"

Vander was relived and looked at Devon in his arms from their positon on the floor. "Are you okay?"

"Yeah, I'm fine."

He let out a nervous laugh. "You nearly got yourself killed with that game you were playing," Vander announced. "What made you think to pull such a crazy stunt?"

Devon hid her smile from him. "You wouldn't believe me if I told you."

Vander studied her a moment, smiled, and clung to her. Dino slowly pulled himself to his hands and knees not far from them. He looked defeated and completely worn.

"What do we do with him?" Ravin asked.

Tyson painfully approached his battered uncle and studied him where he remained on his hands and knees. "I have an idea," Tyson informed them while tilting his head to the side and smirked. "It's a little crazy, but hear me out--"

Tyson raised the ax and severed Dino's head from his body. Blood spattered both Vander and Devon's faces where they kneeled on the floor. Dino's body collapsed as his head rolled across the floor. There were several gasps.

Tyson tossed the bloodied ax aside, grinned proudly, and shrugged. "Problem solved."

Vander clung to Devon to the point of suffocating her and stared at Dino's severed head on the floor not far from him. "I'm glad I didn't see that," Vander muttered.

"Yeah, me too," Novak gasped with horror.

Devon helped Vander to his feet and stared at Dino's body then looked at his spirit. Dino's spirit straightened, stared down at his headless body, and then looked back at Devon. He seemed surprised that she saw him. He opened his mouth to speak. Devon glanced at more than one hundred ghosts standing just behind him. Dino noticed her gaze and slowly looked behind him. The ghosts swarmed around him, clutching and grasping before finally engulfing him as he screamed in terror. Devon hid her smile, shut her eyes, and clung to Vander.

✝

*T*he Fox Ridge Village Hotel had been abandoned for a few years and showed signs of much needed repairs. Its elegant exterior was in need of paint and several windows were broken while lower windows were boarded. Tall grass covered the once lavishly landscaped resort grounds, and vines seemingly grew from the hotel's exterior and covered the first two floors. A dilapidated realtor's sign leaned severely and swayed in the breeze with a bold 'sold' plastered across the front. A backhoe sat alongside the hotel in preparation to level it. Ghostly laughter was heard echoing from within the hotel walls. The Marlins' terrified screams soon followed.

The End

Dead Village

Other books by Holly Copella!
Reviews left on Amazon are appreciated!

"The Battle for Andrea Maria"

A cruise ship attack turns six survivors into overnight celebrities after they take credit for the heroic act of a stowaway who died saving them.

The cruise is just what Jess needed--a bit of harmless fun far from her daily grind. But what begins as a relaxing vacation turns into a desperate fight for her life when terrorists take over the ship and start piling up bodies. Teaming up with a mysterious stowaway, Jess attempts to send out a distress call but knows they cannot wait for help to come. If she or the few remaining passengers have any hope for survival, Jess must act now. The papers dub it "The Battle for *Andrea Maria*," but to Jess it is the moment she fought side-by-side with her enigmatic Romeo, saving the ship--and losing him. She thinks the story ends there, but really, the nightmare is just beginning...

"Insanely Deadly"

When the dead return to life, it's up to an admiral's daughter and a mildly insane, former war hero to save their small town.

Jetta Cross, a Navy Admiral's daughter, is tasked with keeping her father's comrade, a former war hero turned town crazy, grounded in the real world. Capt. John Hunter is still fighting the war in his head, where imaginary dead people are part of his world. When a viral outbreak brings about a zombie uprising, Hunter is left to his own devices. He must resume his role as a one-man commando unit in order to destroy the ravenous undead. With Hunter still fighting his own inner demons as well as the undead, the townspeople fear their zombie neighbors may not be the only threat. Stranded at the island's luxurious resort with a handful of workers, Jetta is forced to live up to her father's reputation and take charge of the deteriorating situation at the hotel. She must wage her own war against the infected before the government declares her hometown a total loss.

"Deadly Institution"

A town recluse suspected of killing his wife teams up with a young woman in order to stop a killer.

After being accused of murdering his wife, Konrad Asher turns his back on the town that once adored him. Ten years later, he still holds his grudge and the title of the most feared man in town. With the reopening of the burned mental institution, where his wife had died, former employees are now murdered one-by-one, throwing suspicion back on Asher. A young local reporter, Jacey, is forced to reveal her long-time friendship with the infamous recluse in order to clear his name not only in the recent murders but to exonerate him in the death of his wife as well. Will Jacey's relationship with Asher invite the killer closer to her? Or is the killer already in her life?

"Screenplays: The Island Collection"
"Jungle Princess", "A.L.F. Resort", "Brighton Island"

Discover how romance and fun in the sun can be downright *chilling*!

"Jungle Princess" is a romantic/thriller that leaves a teenage girl stranded on an island with two male shipmates and a creature of "unknown" origin. She soon discovers the island is home to an abandoned prison with several prisoners roaming free. What really killed over one hundred prisoners? And is it still out there--?

"A.L.F. Resort" is a romantic/thriller set on an island resort with Artificial Life Forms as the main draw. At this resort, all your fantasies come true...until a malfunction removes safety inhibitors on the A.L.F.'s. Zombies, biker gangs, and mobsters run amuck, turning fantasies into nightmares. A young reporter gets more of a story than she anticipates, but will she survive long enough to write the story?

"Brighton Island" is a romantic/thriller set on a private island. When the owner's niece brings her psychic friend to the mansion, his presence awakens the spirits' tortured souls. As the psychic attempts to solve the old murders, the niece is confronted with the possibility that she's next to join the mansion ghosts. Stranded on the island with a crazed killer, her uncle wages his own war to save them. Will his "shock and awe" tactics actually save them or get them killed?

"Town Darling"

After surviving a brutal attack that claims the lives of those she loves, a young woman seeks revenge on a corrupt town.

Going back home is never easy, but for Casey, it means returning to her corrupt hometown where she barely survived a brutal attack. Accompanied by two *family friends*, she seeks justice for the night that destroyed her life. Her physical scars are nothing compared to her emotional ones, forcing the local sheriff to believe that the town darling is back for revenge. As the conspiracy for her revenge appears to be leading up to the coveted town fair, the sheriff is determined to stop her from fulfilling her vengeful scheme...but guilt over his role on that fateful night continues to haunt him. His desperate need for Casey's forgiveness could be his undoing.

"Death Displacement"

A grief-stricken man travels back in time to seek revenge on the woman who murdered his girlfriend but inadvertently falls in love with her.

Kane is about to marry the woman he loves. His life is perfect. A few weeks before the wedding, a vindictive woman from his girlfriend's past mysteriously arrives and kills her. He learns of a traumatic accident that happened five years earlier, which triggers Riley's hatred for his girlfriend. Distraught over his girlfriend's death, Kane uses an antique time machine to travel into the past in order to find and destroy the woman responsible. When he runs into Riley's younger self, he realizes she's not the monster she later becomes, and he can't bring himself to destroy her. With a little help from his oddball friend from the past, they formulate a plan to prevent the accident that sends Riley down her destructive path. Kane's plan backfires when he falls for the younger Riley. His new tortured existence is further complicated when future Riley, his girlfriend's killer, shows up with her own devious agenda that doesn't include him. Will he be able to stop the time ripple, which ultimately ends with his girlfriend's death? Or will future Riley take him out of the timeline forever--

"Reaper of Souls" A fantasy short story

A young woman must outwit an evil sorcerer in order to save her brother or become one of his minions forever.

Unwilling to believe her brother is dead, Reggie discovers an underhanded deal made with Kahn, a less than ethical sorcerer, who collects humans to serve as slaves in his kingdom. In order to rescue her brother from his horrible fate, she must complete his failed task or be forced to serve Kahn forever. After being transported to his world, Reggie realizes that even if she beats Kahn at his own game, she's at his mercy for him to uphold his end of the deal. All seems lost until Kahn's discontented, self-serving brother, Helsing, arrives. Can Reggie convince Helsing to help her? And at what cost?

Coming Soon!

"Basement Dwellers"

A viral outbreak at a hospital leaves a mortician, sheriff, and coroner fighting for their lives against a horde of undead and the CDC.

"Witness Protection"

After witnessing an execution, a resourceful young woman attempts to disappear while being pursued by a hitman and a handsome federal agent.

ABOUT THE AUTHOR

Holly Copella has been writing since the age of twelve when her frustration at a book's poor plot drove her to author her own story. Over the last decade, she's written a number of screenplays, some of which she's now adapting into novels. Her fascination with zombies and other darker material lends an edge to her writing, which tends to lean toward horror. As a fan of Agatha Christie, she appreciates the craft of a good plot and the importance of creating significant characters.

Hailing from Pennsylvania, Copella lives in the Endless Mountains on a farm with her rescue horses and other animals. In addition to writing and reading fiction, she enjoys riding horses and traveling to Las Vegas and Disney World.